Skateboard Shakedown

Lesley Choyce

Formac Publishing Company Limited
Halifax, Nova Scotia 1993

Cover illustration: Mike Little

Canadian Cataloguing in Publication Data
Choyce, Lesley, 1951-
  Skateboard Shakedown
  ISBN 0-88780-232-X

I. Title
PS8555.H69S52   1989   jC813'.54
C89-098655-X
P27.C46Sk 1989

Published with the assistance of the Nova Scotia Department of Tourism and Culture

Formac Publishing Company Limited
5502 Atlantic Street
Halifax, Nova Scotia
B3H 1G4

Printed and bound in Canada

Contents

Chapter One

The Other Side of the Grave

Gary tugged at the kneepads to make sure they were in place. He put one foot on the skateboard and nervously rolled it back and forth. Right in front of him was the drop-off, the rim of the empty, abandoned swimming pool. He could picture the steep, sloping curve of the wall but he couldn't see it clearly. It was ten o'clock at night. There was just a sliver of a moon that gave the whole scene an eerie glow.

I'm going to get myself killed, he thought. I won't be able to see where I'm going.

Gary had been chased out of here twice this week. It was rotten luck. He had just about got the hang of it. Now they patrolled the place all day long so he had to come back at night.

Pretty soon the town would have the bulldozers come and ruin this place for-

1

ever. It would be just another shopping centre, just another flat parking lot.

Gary had never done this before in the dark. He'd have to do it on instinct. Gary didn't care if he got hurt. He didn't care that if he messed up it would be a long, hard fall onto solid concrete. What he cared about was the thrill of the drop, the speed at the bottom and the rocket ride up the other side. So what if he couldn't see a blasted thing.

Gary heard a noise behind him, a car pulling into the parking lot.

He inched forward and let the nose of the board dangle over the edge. The other kids called this place "the Grave." Tonight that word fit better than ever. Trying not to think about anything, Gary crouched down. He pushed off.

It was like someone had yanked him by the ankles. He was flying down toward the bottom of the empty pool. He was still on his board. The wheels were spinning like crazy. He felt free, alive. And then he felt the slope change. His board had found the curved bottom of the pool but he hadn't slowed down.

And then came the wall. He was rocketing upward now, his feet still planted firmly. One hand held onto the rail. Gary hoped that he would launch right up into space. Instead, he rode high up toward the edge and just as the energy was running out, he carved a turn. His board responded like it was part of his body. Together they dove for the bottom of the empty pool again.

Now somebody was shining a flashlight on him. Now he was in real trouble. His wheels hit some stones and he almost lost balance. A voice was yelling at him, "Are you out of your mind?"

Just maybe, he thought, I have enough juice left to shoot up to the top one more time. If he could zoom up to the ledge, he'd be on the other side of the pool, the other side of the Grave. He went for it.

The wall was right where he expected it. He could feel freedom written all over it. He shot straight up to the top of the wall. Then with one hand on the board, he clawed at the air. His feet tried to find their way back onto the level concrete sidewalk. But something had gone wrong.

His toes caught on the edge of the pool. Instead of diving forward into the bushes as planned, he was spinning backwards. Gary knew exactly what it was going to feel like. The seconds stretched out as he fell through the darkness.

"Look out, kid!" the voice yelled. His flashlight beam caught Gary square in the eyeball as he crashed on the bottom.

Pain. He had landed on his elbows. He had forgotten to wear his elbow pads. His backside had taken the worst of it, though. And his shoulders smashed hard, too. Gary felt like he had just been run over by a school bus. Above him, two men were now shouting. He heard feet on the ladder climbing down to him.

More than anything, Gary wanted to get up and run away. He didn't want to get his parents involved. He didn't want any more hassles from anyone. Nothing was broken. He reached around him in the darkness for his board but couldn't find it. Suddenly, a light was aimed full in his face. He was being lifted to his feet.

"Not you again," said the voice. Gary could barely make out that it was a cop. "Kid, you must have a screw loose or somethin'." Then he paused. "Are you all right?"

"I'm OK," Gary said, trying to make himself sound tough.

"Come on then. This time you come with us to the station. We're calling your parents."

4

Chapter Two

Skatedog in the Night

This was Gary's first time inside a police car. The radio was crackling. There was a rifle mounted upright in the front seat. The man driving was Glenn Foster's old man. The other cop was the one the guys called Duck, short for Donald Duck because his name was Donald Tuck. Duck had turned nicer since they had hauled Gary into the car.

"I don't believe what you were doing, kid," he repeated for maybe the eighth time. Then he turned to Foster and said, "Like, I mean, this idiot was like hanging upside down in mid-air."

"I was just doing a cutback," Gary corrected him.

"Cutback, nothin'," Foster said. "You were flyin'."

Gary smiled and sank back into the seat. He checked to see if his elbow had stopped bleeding. Already the blood had caked up nicely but not before it had left a dark stain on the back seat. He closed his eyes and winced from the pain. Gary noticed that the car smelled like his old man's after shave. *Old Spice*. Yukko.

At the police station Gary was introduced to a pay phone. Foster handed him a quarter. Both men went off in search of coffee. Nobody seemed too worried that he would try to escape. Gary was just a skateboard freak, a skatedog. Nothing more.

The first time they caught him at the pool, he had acted tough. "Hey, man," he said. "Let go of the wheels. That's my board. Skateboarding is my life." But he was just talking tough because Sheila had been there. *Skateboarding is my life*. No. *Skateboarding and Sheila*.

Gary dropped the quarter in the slot. He dialled the number, but it wasn't the number of his house.

"Hello?" a groggy voice answered the phone.

"Hi, Sheila. It's me."

"Hi, Gary. What are you doing calling so late?"

"I got busted at the pool."

"Oh no. Your parents are gonna kill you."

"I know." Gary had been trying not to think about them. Now his heart was pounding. "Sheila, what am I going to do?"

"Just hang tight. I'll come over. Do you need, like, money for bail or something?"

"I don't know. I'm not sure I've been arrested. All they could get me for is trespassing."

"Well, just don't call anyone. I'll come over." And she hung up.

Gary wondered what she had in mind. He sat down on a bench. Foster and Duck came back with coffee and food. They offered Gary a hot dog.

"Thanks." He wolfed it down in three bites.

"Did you get hold of anyone?"

"Yeah," Gary answered. "Someone's coming over." He had no idea what would happen when a fifteen-year-old girl arrived to bail him out.

The two cops sat on either side of him, slurping and chewing. Duck belched loudly.

"Can I have my board back?"

"If you promise to stay out of the pool. You're gonna kill yourself in there. I mean, you can't go diving into a pool if it doesn't have any water."

"I'll stay out of the pool," Gary lied. Trying to stay away from skating inside the pool would be like trying to live without oxygen.

Twenty minutes later Sheila arrived. She didn't see Gary sitting by the phone. Instead, she walked straight up to the desk and demanded to see Gary Sutherland. The dispatcher, dozing behind his microphone, looked up in amazement. Gary sat silently, looking at Sheila. She was beautiful.

Sheila was dressed to the teeth. And she had on makeup that made her look maybe twenty years old. Her voice was full of fire.

"Hey, what *is* this?" Duck asked Gary. "I thought you called your parents."

Gary shrugged. Sheila saw him now, sitting battered and bloody on the bench. She rushed over to him, bent down and kissed him on the cheek, whispering at the same time, "Pretend I'm your older sister." Good old Sheila.

"Hey, sis. Thanks for coming by," he faked. Duck and Foster were staring at the streak of lipstick smeared halfway across Gary's face.

"If that's your sister, I'll eat my badge," Foster said.

Gary was flabbergasted. He had never seen Sheila look so...so old before... and so sophisticated. The girl had guts. She looked Duck right in the eye. "What is my brother being charged with?"

"Well, we haven't laid charges. He was trespassing but..."

"But if he hasn't been charged with anything, he's free to go." It was a statement, not a question.

"Well, yes, but..."

"But I drove all the way over here to get my brother home. He's got school in the morning. And a test in geometry."

Gary was eating it all up. This was great. Geometry? He didn't take geometry. Sheila was working on an Academy Award for Best Actress.

"Let's go, Gary." Sheila grabbed him by the elbow, the bloody one. He squelched a yelp. Together they started toward the door.

"What about my board?" Gary whispered to Sheila. They were almost at the door. He was almost free but he couldn't leave without his board.

Sheila left him standing by the door. She turned back to the policemen. "I believe you have some of my brother's private property. Could we have it back, please?"

The sleepy dispatcher had now been roused to full alert. He was smiling and holding out Gary's most prized possession.

"Thank you," Sheila said.

"You're welcome, ma'am," the dispatcher teased.

Together, Gary and Sheila marched out the front door. Outside in the crisp dark night, she sighed with relief.

"You were incredible," Gary said. "Let's get out of here quick before they change their minds." He took her arm and started to lead her down the street.

"Wait, stupid. I got the car."

"You what?" Gary screamed.

"I borrowed my father's car."

"You stole it!"

"Not so loud. I borrowed it. C'mon, let's go."

"I don't believe this. Since when can you drive?"

"It's not so hard. You'll see."

They got into Mr. Holman's Plymouth. She started up the car and put it in gear. The car lurched forward and she hit the power brakes several times before making a jackrabbit take-off, right in front of the police station.

Gary sat silently, watching Sheila drive. It was really weird. She really did look old. And she had come through just when he needed her.

"What if your father realizes you took his wheels?"

"Don't worry. He was watching baseball and drinking all night. He's conked out by now."

"Well, just in case he isn't, let's get this car back in the driveway. Then you go in. I'll stay outside and watch. Make sure everything is OK. OK?"

"OK." Sheila smiled straight at Gary. It was the look she gave him when she let her tough side down.

"Look out!" Gary screamed at her. A cat was running across the street.

Sheila slammed on the brakes and the car skidded to a halt, then stalled. Sheila looked shaken.

"Want me to drive?" Gary asked. He'd never driven a car in his life.

"You don't have a licence."

"Neither do you," Gary answered. Sheila started up the Plymouth again and drove on.

Gary sank down in the seat. "It was unbelievable at the Grave. You should have been there."

"You didn't invite me."

"It was dark. I thought you'd be scared."

"I'm not scared of anything," she answered defiantly.

"I should know that."

"Besides, I think I'm about ready for the Grave. I put some new wheels on my board. I think I'm ready to graduate from parking lots."

Turning into the driveway, Sheila almost managed to miss the flower bed but not before she had knocked over the trash can. After a few tries, she placed the car in the exact position in the driveway where it had been before. She turned off the motor. "Whew."

Gary leaned over to kiss her. "I have to get in the house," she said and ran for the door.

Gary quietly got out of the car and tiptoed after her toward the house. He pushed through some trimmed bushes and got a clear view into the living-room. She was right. Her father was asleep in front of the TV set. Gary watched as Sheila disappeared upstairs.

Dogs were barking next door as he climbed out from behind the bushes. He ran for the sidewalk and pushed off on his board. All in all it had been a very radical night. Down each new street he turned, more dogs started barking. A few porch lights lit up. Gary felt better than he'd ever felt before. And he knew he was in love with the most wonderful girl on the planet.

He cruised down behind the Big Dipper Shopping Centre, along the sloped parking lot. He cut to the top, then back down, building up momentum. One more trick for the night. One more move before calling it quits.

Gary gave it three good strokes with the foot, then tucked down low, pulled in tight along the wall behind the No Frills store. Up ahead was the sloped loading ramp. The place was lit up with powerful mercury lights. They gave an eerie bronze tint to everything.

Finally he shot up the loading ramp, as he had done many times before. Now if his luck held...

At the top of the ramp he kept going. He was up over the top and out into the air. Getting air time for the second time tonight, he thought. And looking for a place to land.

He found it.

The giant green garbage bin was open, thankfully. His aim had been good. Gary crashed down on top of week-old lettuce and rotting broccoli stalks. He felt tomatoes and cucumbers explode as he landed. Gary didn't mind the garbage at all. In fact, he felt great.

Chapter Three

Gary Forever

When Gary opened the door to his house, his parents were right there, waiting for him.

"I can explain," he said.

His parents took one look at the skateboard, the blood on his elbows and, immediately, Gary knew he was in up to his neck.

"What's that green stuff all over you?" his mother asked.

"Oh, I just slipped on some grass." How could he explain about the exploding cucumbers? How could he explain anything?

"But what on earth is that smell?" asked his father, waving a hand in front of his nose.

Gary shrugged like he had no idea what he was talking about. He saw that his mother was about to go off like a firecracker but his father was trying to be cool.

"Gary, what about your elbow. Are you hurt?"

"It's nothing."

"Nothing!" his mother screamed. "You could have been killed by the looks of it. Or ruined for life!"

This was one of her favourite expressions—ruined for life. Gary never knew exactly what it meant.

"I'm okay," was all he could bring himself to say.

"But this has got to stop," his father stated flatly.

"It's all because of that...that thing." Gary's mom was pointing at his board. "We're getting rid of it, right now."

Gary tucked his board to his chest.

"Look, why don't we discuss this in the morning. Gary, get cleaned up and go to bed." Gary's father was trying to be reasonable again. He had his arm around his wife. Gary jumped at the chance for escape and headed upstairs.

At breakfast Gary wanted to be honest. He wanted to tell the entire story of last night, but his instincts told him to keep his mouth shut.

His father spoke first. "You know how your mother feels about skateboarding. We've also heard that skateboarders are getting a pretty bad reputation in town...fights, all sorts of things."

"Fights? No way. We never get into fights."

"Well, I hope that's true," replied his father.

"Gary, we just don't want to see you get messed up and ruin your life," his mother reminded him.

"Mom, I'm not ruining my life."

"We really should take away your skateboard, you know?" his father said.

Gary stared down into his soggy cornflakes.

"But I don't want to do it." his father continued. "Believe it or not, I think I know how you feel. But I think we need to come to a new understanding. We need some new rules."

His mother made the first one. "In the house by nine o'clock, right?"

"Right." Gary decided he could handle that.

"No fights."

"Check."

"No dangerous stuff on your skateboard."

"Right." He'd wear his elbow pads next time.

His father had the last point. "And if you have any problems, anything, we want you to share them with us. We want to help. You have to be completely up front about it."

"Sure, no sweat." The last point actually seemed like the toughest. He couldn't quite figure out why his parents weren't being harder on him. He felt like he wasn't being punished at all and this made him feel guilty.

His father was looking at his watch. "Geez, look at the time. C'mon, I'll drop you off at school."

Gary grabbed his board and followed his father to the car.

He arrived just five minutes late for homeroom. No big deal. Miss Stephano raised her eyebrows at his arrival but said nothing. They liked each other. Gary never gave her a hard time and she never came down on his case.

Gary sat down and looked around. Meeker gave him a thumbs up. Meeker was reading a science fiction novel. Blades was just combing his hair back, like he did every other day, twenty-four hours a day. When he saw Gary looking at him, he shook some dandruff out onto the back of the kid sitting in front of him. Behind Blades the seat was empty.

Sheila wasn't there. Gary's thoughts froze. He tried not to jump to conclusions. She probably overslept. Gary looked down at his math book and began fidgeting with the pages.

Just then the Faulk came on over the P.A. announcing that lockers would be inspected today.

"They better be clean or I'm handing out detentions. Some of you have had fair warning."

Gary and Meeker hadn't cleaned out their locker all year. It was full of half-rotted sneakers, busted jock-straps, worn out skateboard wheels and assorted spare parts of living. They were probably in for trouble.

"I also want to remind you that students are not allowed in the woods behind the school. Not during lunch. Not before school. Not after school. We've had reports of what's been going on back there..." Blades led the class in a loud cheer of boos, until Miss Stephano stood up and gave the evil eye.

Sheila and Gary had first met in the woods. It seemed like ages ago. They were just kids then. Gary was just walking through on his way to nowhere as usual. Sheila was sitting on a log, smoking a cigarette. She offered him one and he accepted, his first. Sheila struck a match and held it close to his face. The tobacco caught. Gary took a long, deep drag. He held it in, not knowing what to do with the smoke in his lungs. Then he coughed so hard that he fell over on the ground.

"This is great stuff," he said to her, barely able to make his voice work. Sheila laughed and laughed. That was it. Gary never took another drag, but the two of them became great friends. Both were loners. Both hated the same creeps at school—the older, nastier slobs like Stewart Martin, Grange McPhail and Karen Gallagher.

Most girls didn't pay any attention to Gary. Gary was just another skate freak to them. But Sheila treated him like he was the only kid in the world who mattered. She bought him little things that he didn't need. She helped him when he got stuck in the middle of writing a homework project on the Crusades. That part was really weird. Sheila got much worse grades than he did. Yet when she helped him, he ended up with an A instead of a C+.

If Gary hadn't known Sheila up close, he might have thought she was the toughest darn girl in school. She had some old feud going with Karen Gallagher. They lived across the street from each other and Karen had a bad habit of telling Sheila's mother things she wasn't supposed to know...like the fact that Sheila was kissing Gary at his locker...or that Sheila had been caught smoking outside the school by Mr. Faulkner.

When Sheila ran away for the first time, it was after her mother caught her smoking on the back porch. Her mother told her father, and her father turned into a grizzly bear. Sheila turned into a rabbit and ran for cover.

Gary was the one who found her in the woods behind the school. She was sitting all alone under a big spruce tree. Her legs were tucked up under her chin and she had a raincoat held over her head trying to keep dry in a drizzling rain.

"I think I want to go home, now," she said when Gary found her. "But only if you go in with me," she said.

"Sure, let's go," Gary answered and walked her home. "Have to go home some time."

The bell rang. Still no Sheila. Had her joyride to his rescue put her in hot water after all? Gary decided to cut first period French and call her. What did he care about French verbs or the names of the provinces of France? He reached in his pocket and found nothing but lint. Then he remembered the phone on the janitor's desk in the furnace room. He ran through the mob of kids and took the steps into the basement. Rats. The door was locked. Gary dug his hand into his back pocket.

He found the laminated photograph of Sheila, the one he carried everywhere. It had survived his worst wipeouts.

He stared at the photograph and the inscription: *To Gary Forever*, as if that was his name, Gary Forever. It was a joke between themselves.

He slipped the photograph in over the lock and slid it down. No problem. The door clicked open. Inside, he flicked on the light, heard the rumble of the massive heater. He jumped to the phone and punched in the number.

Mrs. Holman answered.

"Hi. Is Sheila there?"

"No, she's in school. Gary, is that you?" Mrs. Holman sounded angry.

"Yeah, it's me. But I was calling because..." He wanted to say because she wasn't in school, but he didn't know if he should say it.

Mrs. Holman already figured out what he was about to say. "She'll be there. She's just late. Her father's driving her. It's your fault, Gary."

"Mine?" He decided to play innocent.

"What were you doing last night, anyway?"

"Skateboarding, that's all."

"Really? I'm not sure I can believe anything you say. But I'll tell you this. Sheila is late for school because her father and I

21

had a long talk with her this morning. She's not allowed to see you again, outside of school, until you clean up your act."

"What? Why? That's not fair."

"We just think you're a bad influence. I'm sorry." Mrs. Holman hung up.

Gary felt like someone had just taken a knife and stuck it in his stomach.

Chapter Four

Empty Hallways, Empty Dreams

Just then Guy Miller, the janitor, opened the door. He was startled at first, then looked back at the lock.

"You, buddy, have a habit of showing up where you don't belong." It was spoken as a fact, not a threat.

"I know," Gary said. "I'm sorry."

Miller went about his business, opening up a tool box, rattling around some tools. "You haven't seen my ratchet set?"

"No. Look, I'm sorry I'm here. I had to use the phone."

"Yeah, yeah. Don't worry about it. Shouldn't you be in class?"

"Right." Gary walked out but not before Miller turned and grabbed him by the shoulders.

"I like you, kid. So don't get in no trouble, hear?" The janitor punched him playfully on the shoulder. Gary walked out into the empty hallway.

Trouble seemed to be all he had. Now he was late for French. Who cares? If he knew in which direction to go, he'd split right now. He'd go find Sheila. But he didn't have a clue. Sheila had more secrets than Pepsi had TV commercials.

He eased open the door to Mr. LaPierre's classroom and slinked in. LaPierre watched but said nothing to him. He kept on rattling off verbs. *"Répétez,"* he'd say. The class repeated after him.

Almost as quickly as he sat down, Gary's thoughts started to drift. Not skateboarding this time. Sheila.

LaPierre was calling on students now.

"Monsieur Blades. What is the past participle of 'to love'?" LaPierre had an exaggerated way of pronouncing people's names and he always used *monsieur* or *mademoiselle.*

Blades didn't respond. He was already fast asleep in the back row. A glistening droplet of drool hung from his open mouth as his head rested on his elbow. The class watched the familiar ritual as LaPierre played it out to the end. *"Monsieur* Blades, are you still alive?" The class chuckled.

Finally, Meeker reached over and flicked Blades on the wrist with a plastic ruler.

Blades' head fell forward until it hit the desk.

"Huh?" Howie Blades' head popped up and he looked around wondering what planet he was on.

LaPierre let the joke play itself out and looked for another victim.

"*Monsieur* Sutherland, what about you? Past participle of 'to love'?"

It was there on the tip of his tongue, but Gary's brain was full of other things. He felt stunned by the question, by the silence. Somebody giggled.

The door opened and Sheila walked in. Her eyes found Gary's but she quickly looked down at the floor. She sat down at a desk by the door.

"*Je t'aime*," Gary said out loud. He was looking at Sheila. But she did not look back.

"Surely, Mr. Sutherland, you don't mean you love *me*? I was asking for the past participle, nothing more."

LaPierre was good at poking fun of kids' mistakes without cruelty. He turned to the frizzy-haired girl in the back row. "Perhaps, *mademoiselle*, you could help *Monsieur* Sutherland with his verb..."

The class dragged. Gary felt like someone had lifted a ton of steel off his head. He sat looking at Sheila's back. Thank God she was here. She never turned around during the entire period. When asked by LaPierre for her homework, she said she forgot it. Gary dutifully handed his in. He had worked on it before his late night skateboard adventure at the Grave.

Ten years passed. Then the bell rang. Sheila got up and walked to the door. Gary ran to catch her.

"I'm sorry I got you into trouble last night," he said.

"It was my decision to take the car. That was pretty dumb."

"Dumb? That was incredible. You saved my life. They might have me in prison now if it wasn't for you." Gary liked to exaggerate.

"Look, Gary, my parents found out about last night. They said they don't want me to see you. I told them I couldn't just shut you out of my life. It was like World War Three at breakfast."

"Maybe I could talk to them."

"I don't know if that's a good idea."

The bell rang. Sheila gave Gary a kiss on the cheek and ran off down the hallway.

He didn't go to his World History class. Guy Miller walked by pushing a bucket and mop but all he said was, "Kid threw-up in 213. Guess who's got to clean it up?" He rolled the bucket on down the hall and around the corner, past where the principal was opening lockers.

The official inspection had begun. As each metal door opened, books, radios, sneakers and assorted garbage fell out into the hallway. "It's just like a pig sty," Gary could hear the principal muttering. Gary knew he better drift further down the hall and around the corner if he was to stay out of Faulkner's way.

The hallway was starting to thin again. It was like the tide going in and out every forty minutes. Gary was alone. He was thinking about the dream. Not something he dreamed when he was asleep. The one he had when he was most fully awake. *The* dream. The one that had him dropping in perfect freefall down the side of the pool, the one that had him shooting up again on the smooth, steep wall, then diving far up into the beautiful empty sky. The one where he landed safely on the surface of the earth again and found Sheila standing there waiting for him. Waiting for Gary Forever.

Chapter Five

"Save the Grave"

At the end of school, Gary went looking for Sheila again only to see her getting in her mother's car and driving away. Gary had been assigned three days of detention for his locker. The principal had found a heavy-metal comic book in the middle of the chaos. Neither Meeker nor Gary even remembered stuffing it in there. That locker was like a museum of all the unwanted stuff of their lives. Faulkner zeroed right in on the comic book.

The comic had what the principal called "foul language and partially unclad men and women." That was probably what had attracted Meeker or Gary to it in the first place. But it wasn't their fault that the writer used four letter words. (Later, Faulkner would sit in his office and circle the words with a bright yellow marker to use the comic as an example at the PTA meeting.) And it wasn't anybody's fault that the people didn't wear a lot of clothing. Maybe it was quite hot on the planet where they lived. Besides they weren't even people. They were aliens.

"How can you tell an alien in a comic book what to wear?" Meeker had confronted the principal, tagging another day onto his punishment.

Gary knew he couldn't stay for detention. There was too much happening. Hassles over the Grave. Problems with Sheila. The last thing he could handle was death by boredom for two hours after school.

He jumped on his board and headed down the school driveway. He saw some other guys on skateboards shoot down the sliding board, tumbling into the dirt at the bottom. They looked like they were trying to break their necks. They looked like they were having fun. But he wouldn't join them. He suddenly felt old. Too old for his age. He grabbed onto the rear fender of a bicycle as it passed by. Gary let himself get towed along until it was time to turn. He slowed down to a crawl.

He staked out Sheila's house for two hours. He walked casually by at first. Then he cruised up and down the street until cars started honking at him to get out of the way. Finally, he went to the door and rang. Sheila's mother was like ice.

She told him that Sheila was busy doing homework. She told Gary to leave at once.

Gary went home for supper but later returned to Sheila's. It was a quiet evening in the neighbourhood. Gary sat down by a juniper bush and made little tents out of sticks, something he had done when he was maybe five years old.

All was silent in the house. At seven-thirty the light went on in Sheila's room. Gary saw her sit down at her desk and start to cry. Time for action. He stalked across the close-cropped grass of the lawn and tapped on her window.

"God, Gary, what are you doing here?"

"I've been here for hours. I just wanted to make sure you were OK."

"Do I look OK?"

"You look terrible."

"Thanks."

"No, I didn't mean that. You know what I mean."

"Yeah." She started to soften. "Wanna come in?"

"Sure."

"Just don't make any noise."

Sheila removed the screen and Gary climbed through. He sat down on the corner of her bed.

Gary had only been here once before. Then, they had both loved the danger of it all. Now it was different. Gary looked around her room at all the girl things. There was a black-and-white photograph of the two of them in the corner of her mirror. They had squeezed up inside a coin-operated photo booth at the mall. They were making monster faces into the camera.

Sheila watched Gary looking at it and she smiled. A TV was turned on in another part of the house. A baseball game. Nobody else knew he was in Sheila's room.

"You didn't visit the Grave today, did you?" she asked.

"I went by there, but the cops were all over the place. I saw Meeker and Blades running for cover. We might never get the place back now."

"Hey, don't try to tell me you're never going back there."

"Oh, I'll be back alright. But what tears me up is that pretty soon, it'll be gone."

"We don't need another crummy shopping centre." Sheila said. "That was a *public* pool, right? *We* owned that land." Gary could see she had just struck on an idea. "Hey, why not try and stop them from selling it to the developer?"

Gary had never thought about the pool that way. "You know, you're right. We'll go to one of those town meetings and tell those bigshots to let us keep the pool as a skateboard park. Why not?"

Gary saw from the light in Sheila's eyes that she was as excited about the idea as he was. It was all part of the dream somehow. The four wheels in the air cutback, the smooth perfect arc of the concrete, the feeling of freedom, independence, and even power. Why not fight for something you believe in as if your dreams really matter?

Gary looked deep into Sheila's eyes. The old Sheila had returned — the one who was full of fire and wise beyond her years.

"Let's go over and visit Rinehart, the mayor. He lives two doors down on the other side—the big house with the swimming pool. We can ask him why we can't keep the old pool as a... skateboard park, like the one over in Westfield. Anyway, I know him; he knows my folks."

"Can't hurt to give it a try," Gary said. "Let's call Meeker and Blades and see if they can cruise over. We'll give the dude a show right in his driveway."

They called the others and agreed to meet in fifteen minutes on the street outside the mayor's house. Gary and Sheila climbed out her bedroom window. Sheila left her radio on full blast, and locked her door, to scare away her parents.

It was nearly dark as they approached Mayor Rinehart's front door. When he answered, the first thing he stared at was

Gary's skateboard. But Sheila took control.

"Hi, remember me, Sheila Holman, from two doors down. We've come to see you because of the pool. We don't want to see the pool wrecked. All we have now are parking lots and the streets, and that's dangerous. At least at the pool there are no crazy drivers."

While Sheila presented her impromptu speech, Meeker and Blades were cruising up and down the driveway on their boards, carving cutbacks and kicking their boards high in the air. Every time they came near the house, they would take a look at the back, at the pool, the solarium with the hot tub and the patio where a party was in progress.

"We don't think you should sell the land to a developer. We don't need another mall," Sheila lectured. "We're members of the community too, and we need a place to skateboard."

When she finally paused, Rinehart came over and put a hand on her shoulder.

"Sheila, I think you know that these boys and their skateboards are not good company for a girl like you. I know your parents. They wouldn't want you to be spending your time with them. Look, the land is all but sold. In fact, the man who's buying it is here this evening. We're going to build one fantastic shopping mall. You'll love it...video arcades and everything." He looked at Gary, standing beside Sheila, and spoke in a voice loud enough for Meeker and Blades to hear, "I've already told the Police Chief that I don't want anyone on that land, or near the swimming pool."

Just then a man came out of the shadows of the house. He walked up to Sheila and put out his hand.

"Hi, I'm Bob Langille. You have a lot of guts, young lady. I heard what you said to Cal. You kids know what you want. I'm the developer here who's going to build the shopping centre. How about you all come to the site tomorrow at four o'clock when we are going to be there to look over the plans. We'll show you what we have in mind. You'll love it. I promise. What to do you say, Cal?"

"Yes, sure...of course," mumbled Rinehart. "But no skateboards, understand?"

"OK," replied Sheila, "tomorrow afternoon at four. We'll be there. You show us your plans; and we'll show you ours."

She turned and set off across the street, the three boys following behind. Outside her house they all paused, looked at one another, unable to find the right words.

Sheila gave Gary a long stare and said, "See you at the pool, 4 pm, if not before."

"But we all got detention."

"You'll figure out something."

"But you'll be there too, won't you? At the Grave, I mean?"

"Sure," Sheila said and pecked him lightly on the forehead with a kiss. "Save the Grave."

"Save the Grave," they responded.

Gary checked his watch. Ten minutes to nine. He'd have to move fast to make it home in time. Meanwhile Meeker and Blades skated away into the evening.

Chapter Six

Faulkner's Revenge

The next day Gary arrived in homeroom just as the bell rang. Faulkner was on the P.A. again almost immediately. He had this hang-up about what he called "untidy lockers." The man was really obsessed with order. It sounded like half the school had detention. He added, "Just a reminder to all teachers that you'll be needed to supervise after school today." Miss Stephano rolled her eyes skyward and sighed. Clearly she wasn't happy that she too was going to have to pay for all the dirty lockers in the school.

Then came the clincher. Faulkner started to read off names of those people he wanted to see in his office right after homeroom. If your name was announced it was never for a good reason. It almost certainly meant grief.

"I'd like to see Howie Blades, Richard Meeker and Gary Sutherland in my office right after homeroom." Blades and Meeker looked at each other in wide-eyed shock. What had they been nailed for now? Gary took it with mock resignation. It was probably because he cut out of detention yesterday. Time to pay the piper.

It was a long walk to the principal's office. Meeker realized he had forgotten to zip up his fly. Blades tied his shoelaces for the first time that day and stopped in front of every piece of glass that held his reflection to comb his hair. Gary, whose head seemed to be in the clouds, was trying to figure out a way to explain why he wasn't in detention yesterday and why he *had* to miss it again today. The truth was out of the question.

The school office was a flurry of activity. Mimeograph machines were trundling their way through worksheets, pop quizzes and history tests. "God I love that smell," Meeker said. He had been a fan of the smell of duplicating fluid ever since second grade.

Mr. Faulkner was standing at his door, ready to greet the victims. "Gentlemen. This way please."

They entered the hated office and Faulkner closed the door behind them with a quiet click, like the closing of a coffin.

Faulkner took position standing behind his massive oak desk. At first, he just stood there rattling change in his pants' pockets, waiting for the boys to get nervous.

"Sit down, please." They sat. "Now, let's pretend we're not enemies, OK?" It was a baffling way to start the conversation. Was this some sort of trick?

"Yeah, that's cool," Blades answered. He was trying so hard to be nonchalant that his voice cracked as he spoke.

"I had a phone call this morning," Faulkner continued, "from the mayor."

"The mayor?" Howie asked, wondering what the mayor had to do with his dirty locker.

"It seems that the mayor had some visitors last night."

Faulkner allowed for a long, deathly pause to let the tension mount. Blades squirmed in his seat. Richard looked like he was about to faint. Only Gary seemed resigned to the fact that the entire world was ready to gang up on him. He had guilt written all over his face.

"Perhaps Mr. Blades would like to explain about this business of the abandoned swimming pool?"

Blades was caught completely off guard. "The pool?" His hands flew up in the air.

"What about you, Mr. Meeker?"

Richard was pale and turning green. "I don't know nothin'," was all he could say. He already sounded like a convicted criminal.

"I guess that leaves you, Mr. Sutherland. Tell us about the pool."

Gary was cool. "We call it the Grave," he said. "But that's just a name we gave it. We figured out a while back that an empty swimming pool was a great place to skateboard."

Blades' and Meeker's jaws dropped down to their knees. Faulkner seemed more keenly interested than ever. "Then you do know something about this business the mayor was talking about?"

"Yeah, well sort of," Gary said. There seemed to be no turning back at this point. "You see, an abandoned swimming pool like this one has curved sides that make for unbelievable moves. I mean, this place is the best thing that ever happened to skatedogs in this town, maybe in the whole country."

Faulkner's deep-set eyes tried to pierce right through Gary. The principal's brow was knotted and furrowed. The man was trying to melt Gary down with a death ray. "I see. Now, what about this little meeting you are going to have at the ... er, pool, Mr. Sutherland? "

"Well, this guy Langille, he said we should come to the Grave at four o'clock. He'd show us the shopping centre plans. We were very polite." Gary pointed to Howie and Richard... "We just hope to show the town how important this place is to us. We think it should be saved."

Meeker and Blades just about fell off their seats. One visit to the mayor's house and now it's a big political deal.

"Well, I'm afraid the mayor is more than a little annoyed. He says that land is already sold. The pool will be filled in and work on the new shopping mall starts next month. Besides, he thinks skateboarding in a swimming pool is too dangerous. Someone might get hurt." Faulkner stopped talking and looked up at the ceiling. He seemed confused about something. "Wait a minute. I used to swim in that pool. It's over twenty feet deep in parts."

"Yep."

"You mean, you ride down the wall...?"

"Then cruise across the bottom," Gary interrupted, "and shoot up the other side. If you're good and if you're lucky, you shoot off the lip and you're in mid-air. Then you crank it around and connect with the wall again on the way down. It's not that hard if you know what you're doing."

"Holy Smokes!" Faulkner said, not seeming like a principal at all.

"We wear elbow pads for safety," Meeker suddenly chimed in, trying to make them sound respectable.

Faulkner ignored the elbow pads. "Gary, why didn't you go first to the town council instead of going to the mayor?"

"I just figured that no one else would listen to me."

"So you just decided to have a face-to-face with Rinehart?"

"Well, it wasn't exactly my idea..." But he cut himself off. He decided to leave Sheila out of it. "No, I can't lie. It was my idea. I guess I really screwed-up, huh?"

"Perhaps, yes, perhaps you did." And then the Faulk said a very strange thing. "But I think that it's something you have to see through."

"You do?"

"Well, you got yourself into it and seem to think you know what you're doing. But I have to tell you, I grew up with Mr. Rinehart. He's a very tough cookie. And he doesn't like it when things don't go his way." There was something funny about the way Faulkner said it, something that told Gary that Faulkner really hated Rinehart. Faulkner continued. "You'll have to work hard to convince him to change his plans. And if they tell you to

41

leave, leave. Don't try to put up a fight. Now, I can't stop you from going. It doesn't have anything to do with school, now does it?"

All three of the guys were flabbergasted. Old Faulk seemed to be backing them.

"There is one problem, however. You're all slated for detention today. I *could* keep you here in school. That part *is* my job."

Their spirits sank a mile beneath the floorboards.

"But I won't," he concluded. "You miss today's detention, you owe me three days for it next week. You're not off the hook. But I won't stop you from doing this. Now get out of here and get to class."

Blades, Meeker and Gary were out of the office and down the hall before it sank in that Faulkner had just said something very weird. It had never once in their entire school career occurred to them that Faulkner was actually a human being. Gary's sense of reality was so distorted that he could barely find his way to French class. He had gone so far as to share a fragment of the dream with Faulkner. And Gary had the most bizarre feeling that the principal had actually understood. The world had just done a double backflip and Gary kept waiting for it to come down.

Chapter Seven

The Blueprint

Gary was scared. He didn't know how to confront the mayor. What could he say that could convince Rinehart that the pool was worth saving? Nothing. It would be a joke. The three of them walked around the entire perimeter of the chain link fence.

"Why don't we just go inside like we always do? Rinehart's not gonna show up," Richard said, his voice exposing his jitters.

"Yeah, let's get some air time before we lose the pool altogether. Nobody's gonna listen to us." Howie was the voice of doom.

"Let's just see this through. It's not just the pool. It's our rights." Gary was trying to sound tough. He hadn't really thought about his rights at all. He *did* know that he was royally mad that some idiot in a suit could sign a paper and take away one of the most important things in his life.

So they circled the chain-link perimeter of the pool grounds one more time.

"What happened to Sheila, anyway?" whined Richard. "This was her idea wasn't it? She was the one who got us into this."

"Yeah. I don't know where she is," Gary answered. "I think she's in hot water with her parents. She'll be here if she can."

But maybe she wouldn't be there. Gary couldn't find her after school. Yeah, he thought, she had got them into this. He didn't know how to talk to any mayor. She did the talking yesterday.

Gary watched as a dark car turned in the driveway of the old swimming pool grounds. No. Not one car. Two. The second one was a police car.

"Let's run," Howie said.

"Yeah, let's run," Richard echoed.

"No. I'm staying." Gary heard himself say it even though his instincts told him to get out of there.

So the three of them were just standing there looking incredibly dumb, holding their skateboards to their chests, when the doors of the first car opened. Out stepped Rinehart first, a briefcase in his hand. The creep was laughing at something. Other doors opened. Three other men in business suits stepped out. One of them was Langille. They were all laughing at something but they weren't even looking at the skatedogs.

The cops just sat in their car. Gary heard the static of the radio and the idling car engine.

Rinehart looked over at them but he didn't seem to acknowledge their presence. What was going on?

One of the other men pulled a long rolled up sheet of paper out of the car and spread it out on the hood. The others leaned over as the man pointed at the paper and then around him at the parking lot and the empty pool.

Gary felt numb. He didn't know what to do. Somewhere in the back of his brain he heard the sound of a skateboard cruising on concrete, the clunk of the wheels as it went over cracks in the sidewalk. He figured it was his imagination but Blades and Meeker had already turned to see who it was.

Sheila. Thank God.

She rolled up to the guys and stopped. "What's going on?" she asked.

"I don't know," Gary said. "They don't act like we're here at all."

"So let's go talk to them," Sheila said. "What are you waiting for?"

Gary felt extra dumb. What was he waiting for? He couldn't wimp-out now.

"Yeah, let's talk to them. I have a few things I want to say." Gary knew it was his job to do the face-to-face.

The men were studying something on the paper when they walked up. Gary saw that it was some kind of a plan, a blueprint on the hood of the car. Rinehart was the first to acknowledge their presence. He was smoking a cigarette and sucked in a long hard draw before he spoke.

"Well, Sheila, boys," he said, rivetting his eyes on Sheila, "I'm really glad that we have this opportunity to meet again."

Bob Langille, holding down the blueprint with one hand, held out the other but none of them were willing to shake it.

"I must say that I'm really pleased that you had the courage to express your opinions to me," Rinehart said. The words sounded hollow.

"We want the city to let us use the pool. We don't want you to wreck it." There, Gary blurted it out.

"Son, be reasonable. A situation like this is just too dangerous. You can't ride your skateboards down the wall of an empty swimming pool."

"Why don't you let us show you," Gary said. Sheila nodded her head. Howie and Meeker just said, "Yeah."

46

Rinehart chuckled, inhaled again on his cigarette. The three other men laughed too.

"I can't let you do that. Could you imagine if some parents heard that I stood by and allowed you to break your necks on my account? I'd be run out of town. I'm sorry lads, but your swimming pool days are over. Look, we hope to build a new indoor swimming pool, oh, probably some time in the next six or seven years. As soon as town council approves the money."

"But we're not talking about swimming," Sheila interrupted. "We're talking about skateboarding."

"I've been led to believe by some well-respected parents that skateboarding is not only dangerous but it brings about moral decay in young people."

"Oh, come on," Sheila nearly shouted at him.

"Please, young lady, you were polite last night. You have to understand that there are already plans under way." Rinehart pointed to the blueprints. "Mr. Langille already has an option to buy this land and his men have drawn up a plan for one of the finest shopping malls in the country."

"But we don't want another shopping mall," Gary shouted. He was losing his cool.

"In fact," Rinehart continued, "as I said last night, there'll be a video arcade in the new mall. Something for everybody. Now doesn't that make more sense than wasting this entire piece of property on a few of you who want to get your kicks by trying to break your bones in an empty swimming pool."

"No, it doesn't. We don't want a video arcade. We want a place to skateboard."

Mr. Langille was rolling up the plans. Rinehart was stubbing his cigarette out on the ground. "Perhaps you can come by my office some time next week and we can talk further. I'm sure you'll begin to understand that we only want what's good for the community. And for you as well."

The men got back into the car. "Wait," Sheila demanded, but nobody did anything. The driver of the car spit gravel at them as he pulled away.

The police were still just sitting in their car, waiting for the kids to leave.

"Let's just go inside now and get a few good rides. We'll show those guys who they can push around." It was Howie, talking big.

"Yeah, let's show them who they can push around," Richard added.

"Don't be stupid," Sheila said. "We'd be playing right into their hands. Why do you think he had the police come along?"

"So what do you want us to do? Just give up?" Gary was taking out his frustration on Sheila.

Sheila smiled. "No. I've got another idea. Just give me some time. I've got to get home." She drew Gary aside and whispered, "Come over again tonight at eight thirty. Plan B. We'll show Rinehart who he's messing with."

"Plan B?" Gary asked. But Sheila was already off, cruising down the street on her board towards home.

After dinner, Gary told his parents he was going over to Sheila's. He didn't tell them that he wasn't supposed to see her.

"What will you be doing over there?" his mother asked. Gary's mother always asked him questions that were impossible to answer. He had learned long ago to give very vague answers.

"Not much," he said. But he kept wondering exactly what "not much" would be. He was dying to know what Sheila had in mind for Plan B.

Sheila was waiting for him by her window. When Gary was in she said, "Sit down."

He sat. Sheila picked up the phone book again, found a number and dialled it.

Gary sat silently, waiting ... waiting for Plan B.

"Hello, could I have the newsroom? Yes, thank you."

Gary was bewildered. Sheila looked straight at him and smiled. She looked like she might start to giggle, but she straightened herself when someone came on the line on the other end.

"Hi, you don't know me but I live in the Riverdale section. Do you ever, like, do stories about problems that kids have? Good. Well, we have a problem out here in Riverdale. The city wants to take away the best skateboarding place in town and build a stupid shopping mall and we'd like to stop them."

Gary had the feeling that this was heading towards big trouble. How the heck were kids gonna stop the city from selling land to a developer for a shopping mall?

"No, we're quite serious about this," Sheila said over the phone. "Nobody understands how important this is to us. Kids should have rights too."

Whoever was on the other end seemed to be sympathetic.

"It's an abandoned swimming pool. Skatedogs who go there know what they're doing. If only you could show people on TV how incredible it is, I think we could save the place. Could you meet us there tomorrow at, say, four o'clock?"

Gary couldn't tell from Sheila's reaction whether she was succeeding or not. But he knew it would never work. Besides, he couldn't let his parents see him on TV. They didn't know anything about the Grave. If they saw him dive-bombing down the wall of the deep end, he'd lose his skateboard for sure. Sheila said good-bye and hung up.

"Well?" Gary asked.

"Tomorrow at four. KTV will be there. This lady sounded real cool. Her name's Kelly Merrill. She says she thinks kids should have rights. She thinks it's gonna make a fantastic story."

"Sheila, what have you got us into?" Gary was scared and excited all at once.

Chapter Eight

The Pumphouse Invasion

Howie and Richard thought Plan B was perfect. They loved the idea of going on TV. It was agreed that they would all have to skip detention again and explain to Faulkner afterwards. If it worked, they would be heroes. It would be worth five weeks of detention. Blades went around school trying to enlist a few other skate-dogs. He was in his glory. Gary, however, shouldered more than a few doubts.

At three o'clock when the final bell rang, Gary was sitting in Mr. Wilfred Tingley's English class. Tingley had the bad habit of continuing to lecture after the bell had rung. If he was in the middle of making a point, he would carry on and on. Today's subject was the novel, *Johnny Got His Gun*. Mr. Tingley wanted to make it perfectly clear that the novel was against war, and that he himself was opposed to all war in any way, shape or form. The precious seconds dragged on until at last the man had to stop for air.

Tingley wasn't given a chance to start another word. Immediately, the students were up out of their seats and racing for freedom. Howie and Richard led the pack, dragging Gary along. Gary wanted to hang back and wait for Sheila. He needed to be sure she'd be there at the Grave.

"C'mon, man, we gotta move. She'll come by when she's ready," Blades argued.

"We can't wait," Meeker added.

And so they were out into the bright afternoon sunlight and pushing off for the Grave. Gary tried not to think about Sheila. She promised she'd be there. He didn't want to have to go through this without her.

All three were completely out of breath by the time they saw the pool. There was a cluster of cars in the parking lot. Among them were two town police cruisers and a station wagon with "KTV" written on the side. Gary could see a guy holding onto a shoulder video rig and a young woman pushing a microphone toward a man in a suit—Mayor Rinehart.

"The enemy," Blades said, pointing toward the mayor. "Let's get him."

"Yeah, let's go," Meeker said, sounding tough as nails now.

"Wait a minute. We can't just go running over there like idiots. We need a plan."

"Right," Blades said, always willing to let Gary's good sense have right of way.

Only three of the other skateboarders had arrived...Kyle, Wiser and Jones. They would have to do. There was no time to waste. Gary led them all behind a fence so they wouldn't be spotted.

When he studied the scene, it looked impossible. With the cops around, they would never be able to make it inside the grounds of the pool.

"It's hopeless," Meeker said.

"We'll never have time to get over the fence," Jones added.

"What a waste," Blades concluded. "Let's go home."

"No. I have a plan." Gary pretended to sound like he knew exactly what he was up to; he was faking it. "The cops have the only easy entrance blocked. You can bet they're not gonna let us through there. And what we need to do first is let the TV cameras show us in action. We want people to see what we're trying to save."

"Two guys are going to have to volunteer to provide a distraction. To walk straight up to the cops and ask permission to go in."

Gary looked around at the faces. There was no glory in it. Nobody volunteered.

"Meeker?" Gary asked. "Please?"

Richard was the one most likely to get wasted on his first drop in the pool anyway. He knew it, too. "Yeah, sure," he said, resigned to his fate as low man on the totem pole.

Jones volunteered as well.

"Great," Gary said. "Now circle around and come in from the front. If the TV people start asking questions, just tell them we want the town to give us back the pool. You'll look great on TV."

Gary slapped Meeker and Jones on their backs and sent them off. He suddenly felt like a young kid again. This was all a game, like playing Capture the Flag in Boy Scouts. Gary had been patrol leader of a pack of snotty-nosed, whining kids who somehow turned into expert woodsmen when they played. And they had always won.

"OK. Now, we shoot around behind the pump house. Over there we can get right up to the fence without being seen." Gary looked around him. Blades had on a screaming orange and yellow shirt. Wiser had on mega-red pants and Kyle was wearing white cut-offs, an explosive purple day-glo Adidas T-shirt and mirrored sunglasses.

"When we move from there, we have to be over the fence and to the pool in seconds. Then go for it. Just don't mess up."

"Man, we're gonna be like legends when this is over," said Blades.

"Hey. No heroes," Gary chided. "And look, we make our drop, carve it up and down a few times. Then we stop. When the cops come for us, we don't do anything but what they want."

Not everyone liked the idea, but Gary didn't give anybody a chance to talk. "If we want to make our point, we have to look good on TV. We gotta look cool and together. Check?"

"Check."

"Then let's move."

The four of them made a run through several backyards behind the pool. They charged over a picket fence and landed in somebody's flower bed. Inside the house a lady screamed out something hysterical. She thought she was watching the invasion of some crazy army. They ran on across a patio past a smoking barbecue. They crawled along behind a hedge of juniper shrubs and arrived behind the pump house, wheezing for breath.

Gary studied the top of the eight-foot-high chain-link fence. He studied the rusty knots of jagged steel at the top.

"Ready? Go."

At once they jumped for the fence. Gary's arms moved automatically. He was watching the crowd on the other side. The cops were talking to Meeker and Jones. They were distracted. The TV lady was trying to push a microphone up to Jones. The mayor and the other men in suits looked annoyed. But something was missing. Sheila. Sheila wasn't here. And this was the big moment.

All four jumped down the other side onto the concrete. Kyle had ripped his red pants on the fence. Wiser's sunglasses fell to the pavement and shattered. But the revolution was about to begin.

Gary yelled a command: "Don't run. Walk!"

They walked to the edge of the pool. Their unexpected arrival baffled everyone on the other side of the pool. The cameraman, however, was turning their way and sidling up past the police barricade. Gary found the edge of the pool and set his board on the lip. Kyle, Wiser and Blades were right beside him. Gary announced the beginning of their performance simply with the words, "Ladies and Gentlemen…" And with that they all took the big plunge.

It was a moment of grace and beauty. Each of them was barely attached to his board. The wind whipped past through their straggly hair and the thrill of the drop pulled a shout of "Cowabunga!" out of somebody's mouth.

Then came the softer curve halfway down the side and the arrival at the bottom of the pool, shaped like a giant toilet bowl. Kyle took a left turn at the bottom and began to carve a circular path around the pool, arcing halfway up the wall, then kicking it higher, then lower in crazy, wavy patterns. Blades and Wiser performed a perfect criss-cross as they shot up the other side and together snapped hard cutbacks off the tiles at the top of the pool. As they headed back for the bottom and up the other side, a cheer went up from Meeker and Jones.

The police made their way to the edge of the pool. Foster and Duck were back on the offensive. But while Kyle was swirling around the bowl, Blades and Wiser were on a criss-cross descent.

Gary used all the speed he had gathered to launch himself straight up over the lip and into the air. He rocketed higher than ever before. He was maybe six feet up into the wild blue yonder and everything had turned to slow motion. The cops were yelling. Meeker let out a hoot. The cameraman had moved in close so that he was almost underneath Gary. A feeling of calm and control swept through Gary as he began to fall back to earth. He was beyond the edge of the pool. He reached down and his left hand found the board. His other hand was sailing off wildly into the sky. He could hear the blood pounding in his ears as his body prepared for the shock of the landing.

And then he was down. The world clicked back to normal time. His wheels found the pavement and he was still attached to the board. Still using the forward momentum, Gary rolled slowly to a stop as Foster walked up, grabbed him by the shoulder, and then yanked away the board.

Down in the pit, Duck was still trying to bring the other daredevils to a halt. Miraculously, nobody had wiped out.

A pretty young woman with a microphone made her way to Gary. The mayor was yelling something at her, but she ignored him. She walked up close to Gary but didn't speak directly to him.

"Pull in tight on this," she said to the camera guy. "Okay Chuck...right..." She shoved a microphone up to Gary's face. "Can you tell me who you are and what you're doing here today?"

Foster let go of Gary's shoulder and tried to move off, out of camera range. He didn't want to be in the shot. "I'm Gary Sutherland and I want the town to give us back this place. We call it the Grave but that's just a nickname. It's got the best skateboarding maybe anywhere in the country. It used to be a public pool and it belonged to the people who live in the town. We live here and we want it back. That's all there is to it."

"But isn't it dangerous? That looked like some treacherous drop down the side."

"It's not that bad if you know what you're doing."

"Aren't those scars on your elbows? Have you ever been injured here?"

Gary pulled his elbow pads into place. The question put him off-balance. "Look, ah, I don't quite know how to make you understand this, but if you knew what it felt like to be surfing that concrete wave, you'd say a few cuts and bruises were worth it."

In the background, Gary heard the mayor saying, "All right, that's enough. Get everyone out of here!"

Kelly Merrill turned toward the mayor and gave him a dirty look. Then she turned back to the camera. "So it looks like a show-down between some militant skateboarders and the town officials here in this otherwise placid bedroom community. I'm Kelly Merrill...in Riverdale."

Almost as soon as she had finished talking, she and the cameraman were walking away. The story was over. They were leaving. Duck had rounded up the other guys in the pool. Foster was leading Gary toward Mayor Rinehart. Rinehart looked furious.

"Kid, you're nuts. If you think we're gonna give in to this ridiculous scheme of yours, you have to be out of your mind." Gary said nothing, just watched the man get in his black Lincoln and drive off.

Foster, Duck and two other cops looked at each other and at their prisoners.

"Now what do we do with them?" Duck asked.

"Nothing," Foster said, pointing toward the TV crew that had retreated to the side of their car, still ready for action. "We let 'em go. We try to haul in these kids with the cameras still around and their mommies and daddies are gonna be shouting 'police brutality' up and down the block."

"Let's just walk this way, boys. We just want to start you on your hike home. Be nice and cool now. No trouble. We're on your side, really," Foster said smiling right through the lie. "But we're just gonna hang onto your boards for a while to keep you out of trouble."

And that tiny voice in the back of Gary's brain decided it was time to remind him: *Sheila had never shown up.* Something was wrong, real wrong. How could she set this all up and then not be here?

Chapter Nine

A World of Lies

For once, Gary was home in time for dinner. He saw his mother stir-frying vegetables in the kitchen. His father was reading the paper. Gary slinked into the livingroom and dialled Sheila's number. It rang twelve times but nobody answered. He hung up. But it was driving him nuts. He had to know why Sheila wasn't there today.

His father came into the room. "Anything interesting happen today, Gary?"

"Nah, nothing much. Same old stuff. What about with you?"

"Not much excitement, I guess. Just work, that's all."

"Yeah, I guess it was just one of those days." Gary excused himself and went to the upstairs phone. He dialled Sheila's house again. It rang...seven, eight, nine times. He was just about to give up when Sheila answered the phone.

"Where were you?" he blurted out

"I told you, I'm not allowed to see you," She said. The words cut through him like a knife.

"But you were the one who set it up. They were there...the TV people. We pulled it off. You should have been with us."

"No, I'm sorry Gary, like I said, I can't see you. That's what my parents said and I have to stick by it."

Gary didn't understand. What was going on? He couldn't believe that Sheila had chickened out.

"I've gotta go," Sheila said and hung up.

"Wait!" But all he heard was a dial tone. There was no point in phoning back.

Gary's mother yelled upstairs, "Food's on. C'mon Gary." Gary walked downstairs, the life drained out of him.

"Anything interesting happen today, Gary?" his mother asked as they sat down to a homemade Chinese meal.

"Dad and I have been through that already," he said and began to pick the bean sprouts out of his rice and put them on a pile to one side on his plate.

"Not much of anything interesting, I guess, for either of us," his dad answered.

The phone rang. Gary answered it. It was Blades.

"Can I come over to watch the news at your house? My old man's gotta watch

'Business Today' and the VCR's broke. I don't want to miss it."

"No, you can't. Goodbye." Gary hung up before his parents got the drift that something was up.

But as soon as he sat down, the phone rang again. It was Meeker.

"Gary, I gotta come over to your house to watch the news. I can't let my parents see it. They'd crucify me."

"No way. Sorry. Bye."

Gary tried to sit down and eat as if nothing was happening. His parents were looking at each other. They knew something was up.

Gary realized that he wouldn't be able to sit down and watch the news either without his parents all over him. He never watched the six o'clock news. Now what?

He thought about Sheila. He thought about his two buddies and how they'd let him down too. He had already figured he would go over to one of their houses to watch the news so his parents wouldn't find out. Rats.

"Gary," his father said, "like I told you, if you're in some kind of trouble, we need to know. We want to help." Gary knew that he had guilt written all over his face. But what the heck? He wasn't guilty of anything. And he was getting tired of playing cover up.

"OK, look. I'm not really in trouble. It's just this thing that happened at the Grave."

"The grave?" His mother dropped her fork and the blood drained out of her face.

"You know, the old public swimming pool. It's where we skateboard sometimes."

"He means in the old parking lot," his father assured his mother.

"No," Gary confessed. "In the old pool."

His folks looked baffled. "You'll understand. Just don't go flying off the handle until you see."

"See what?" his mother demanded.

"Is it OK if I invite a few of the guys over to watch the news here tonight? It's on in twenty minutes."

"The news?" His dad asked. "You want to invite your friends over to watch the news on television?"

Gary understood the confusion. "Yeah, the news."

"I guess it's alright," he said. It was like his son had just asked him if it was a problem to get straight As in school.

Gary got on the phone and called Blades and Meeker. They said they'd be right over. Then he tried Sheila but somebody simply lifted up the phone and slammed it down again.

The guys all arrived at once—Blades, Meeker, Wiser and Jones. Gary's mom asked them if they would like some cookies but they just looked at her like she came from Mars.

His father sat down in his usual chair. Everyone else sat on the floor. Nobody spoke. Gary knew he was going to be in trouble when it was all over, but he was still really excited to see himself and the guys carving around the pool.

"I called up everyone I know and told them it was on," Blades said. "Nobody believed me, but they'll all be watching."

"Yeah, so did I," said Wiser.

"Well, this should be interesting," Gary's dad said. He looked really uptight.

The clock said 6:00. Gary clicked on the television to KTV. He saw a really straight-looking dude reporting on something about the Soviet Union, then a story about a shoot-out in a bank, a small earthquake and a jetliner crash.

"Man, this is really boring," Meeker said. "When are they getting to the good stuff?"

"Just shut up and watch," Gary said.

Next came five minutes of commercials: aspirin, Pepsi, processed cheese slices, garage door openers, Coca Cola and car wax. Gary was getting very nervous. He looked at the clock: 6:15.

They sat through more news stories, mostly about politics. The guys were getting restless. Maybe they had bumped the story. Maybe it just wouldn't happen.

6:25. Only five minutes left. The guys were already cheesed-off.

But then it happened. On TV Gary saw a shot of Blades and Wiser doing a criss-cross on the nearly vertical wall of the Grave. And there was Kyle swirling around the curved sides near the bottom. It looked magnificent. Gary gulped and looked at his parents. They seemed stunned.

Over the video footage was the voice of Kelly Merrill.

"Skateboarding is just a pastime for some kids but here in Riverdale, it's serious business..." The next shot showed Gary rising up the wall of the pool from below camera level and he launched over the edge and into the air. But it failed to show his perfect four-point landing. "In fact," Kelly continued, "it's so serious that these four young men are willing to risk their lives daily to get the thrill that they're hooked on..."

No, something was wrong. That wasn't the way it was supposed to go.

"I talked with Gary Sutherland, one of the death-defying skateboarders who says he doesn't mind a few wounds now and then."

Gary saw himself saying, "Look, if you knew what it felt like to be surfing that concrete wave, you'd say a few cuts and bruises were worth it." But they had cut out the rest of the conversation. They weren't telling the whole story!

"Skateboarding like this," Kelly continued, her voice over other film clips of hospital shots of broken bones, bloody gashes and kids with head wounds, "can be very hazardous to your health. So hazardous that the city has decided to fill in this abandoned swimming pool that is a favourite of these young rebels. Here's what Mayor Calvin Rinehart had to say."

A close-up showed Rinehart looking composed and sincere. "I feel that it's my duty to remove this unsafe, and possibly deadly hazard in order to protect the children of the community." He came off on TV as a friendly, concerned guy. The TV people had made Gary look like a reckless kid.

Kelly wrapped up the story saying, "So it looks like Mayor Rinehart will soon have his way and bring an end to this deadly hazard and the kids of Riverdale will just have to find another way to get their kicks."

The room erupted all at once. Everyone was yelling. The guys were furious. Gary's parents were furious.

"They tricked us," Blades said.

"Those rotten turkeys. We'll show them," Wiser fumed.

"Yeah, they made us look like idiots," Blades screamed.

Gary was flabbergasted. But he was worried more about his parents than his friends. Everybody was talking at once. They were blaming him. Gary had enough.

He stood up and screamed. "Just get out of here. Go home!"

The guys stood up and walked to the door. Gary slammed the door behind them. He stood alone in the hallway. His parents were staring at him like he had just committed murder.

"If we had known you were going to that pool, we'd never let you out of the house. Gary, that's too dangerous," his mother said.

"It's not like they made it look."

"But we saw for ourselves," his father said. "You should never have been allowed in there in the first place."

"Then where are we supposed to go? The streets."

"I think you just need to forget about skateboarding," his father snapped back.

"Why? Just because adults don't understand it?"

"There must be something else," his father insisted.

"Think about it. What exactly is there for kids to do around here?"

"There's lots of things. Plenty of sports at school."

"C'mon, give me a break. I'm not into sports. I don't like all that organized stuff. Skateboarding isn't like basketball. It's something you do on your own. You make up your own rules. You don't have to have some coach telling you what to do. You don't understand."

"Well, it sounds like it's all over for the pool, anyway. Not much we can do about that."

"Why not?" Gary snapped back. "Do you think it's right that the city closed down a public swimming pool and is selling the land to a developer? How many shopping malls do we need around here anyway?"

"He's got a point there," Gary's dad admitted to his mother. "Maybe there should be something else for the kids."

"Yeah, you know what Rinehart has in mind? He says there's going to be a video game arcade in the mall. He thinks we should kiss his feet for being so nice to us."

"I don't like the idea of a video arcade, myself," Gary's mother said. "Couldn't he come up with something better than that?"

Gary's father looked thoughtful.

"How come they didn't replace the old pool with a new one anyway?" Gary asked, his anger still boiling.

"Well, I don't really know. They said the city needed the money but...there was talk of a new indoor pool somewhere down the road."

"When?"

"I don't know," his father admitted. "Look, maybe we should talk to the town council about something like a skateboard park. That shouldn't be as much as a swimming pool. And if it was done right, it'd be much safer for kids."

"Sure." Gary sounded sarcastic. "I'm sure that old creep Rinehart will think it's a great idea, for ten years from now."

"Well, I'm going to the next city council meeting to suggest it. Not for ten years away but for now."

"He'll laugh in your face."

"Maybe. But it's worth a try. You're not going to get anywhere by going on TV and making a fool of yourself."

That hurt. He *had* made a fool of himself. He got up to go out of the room. He felt betrayed by everyone. By Kelly Merrill who was supposed to tell his story. By his parents who still didn't understand. But most of all, by Sheila who had got him into this mess.

Chapter Ten

Completely Hopeless, Completely Necessary

At 7:15 the next morning, Gary cut school and caught the bus downtown. He had to talk to the lady at the TV station. The bus was pretty depressing. The people looked like zombies. This was what it would be like to be an adult, Gary thought. You get up every morning and instead of school, you go off to some lousy job. No one looked happy. Most looked barely alive. It made him mad. Why was it that everywhere you turned someone was trying to kill off *fun?* Something out there wanted to stop you from living. You were allowed to breathe, you were allowed to exist but you weren't supposed to *live*. He hugged his skateboard, which he had retrieved late last night from the police station, and tried to forget about the people on the bus.

Two months ago, he had been on this bus with Sheila. Sheila wanted to go downtown to buy some funky old clothes from one of the second-hand stores. Gary had gone along for the ride. They sat together near the back. Sheila held onto his arm and leaned her head on his shoulder.

"You know," Sheila said, "when we get older, we're not going to be like them." She swept her arm around, meaning all of the adults sitting on the bus. "You and I are different."

"We are?" Gary asked. He knew what she meant but he just wanted to hear Sheila talk. He liked it when she made it sound like it was the two of them against the world.

"Yeah. I mean, we don't need anything more than the two of us. If we have each other, we'll have everything we need."

Gary smiled an embarrassed smile. People were listening. Sheila did this to him every once in a while. In public. It was the way Sheila liked to blend 'romantic' with defiant but it always caught Gary off guard. He was supposed to say something too, something loud so everyone would hear, something equally gushy but defiant too. All he could find was the defiant part.

"Yeah," he said out loud, "like we'll never end up like them. The walking dead, the working dead, *The Grateful Dead*." He was almost shouting.

One well-dressed woman turned around and stared at them. Gary just ignored her but Sheila got annoyed. Finally, Sheila made a bizarre face, stuck out her tongue and growled at the woman. The lady never turned around again. Sheila and Gary laughed and laughed.

Today was different. No laughing. And no Sheila. Everyone looked ugly to him. In his wallet he carried the laminated photograph on which she had written, "To Gary Forever."

Gary closed his eyes, breathed in the smell of diesel fumes. The traffic was closing in around them. The streets were becoming jammed. When Miss Stephano took attendance in homeroom, he wouldn't be there. Whenever he showed up at school again, he was sure that Faulkner would be out for blood. Gary wondered what it would be like not to go back. He thought of Sheila again. How many times had he phoned her last night? Twelve times. And nobody even answered. Her parents had finally gotten to her. Maybe she was convinced that he was bad news. If they had seen him on the tube last night, they'd never let Sheila out of the house with him again, ever.

The bus was stopping at every second corner. People filed out. It seemed like people on the sidewalk were running. Everybody was in a hurry to get to where they were supposed to be. The men were all stone-faced. The women wore too much make-up and didn't look real.

Gary looked at his watch, the fancy, over-priced digital "time-piece" his father had bought him. 9:05. He understood why everyone looked so frantic. They were late. They were five minutes late for work. The boss would give them a hard time. Maybe they'd be docked an hour's pay. Gary tried to imagine himself ten years from now. He couldn't. It wouldn't happen.

The bus driver stopped at a light. He turned around and looked at Gary who was now all alone on the bus. "Are you gonna get off or what?"

Gary stood up and hurried toward the front. "Sorry," he said to the driver, "I was daydreaming."

The driver erased his smirk and threw out his arm across the aisle. "If you want, you can just stay on. I'm headed back to Riverdale in twenty minutes." He recognized a kid cutting school, a kid about to get himself into some sort of mess.

"No thanks." Gary had instantly known why the driver had made the offer. He ran for stairs and out into the street.

Almost before his feet touched the sidewalk, he was moving. He was swept along in the swarm of pedestrians now ten minutes late for work and more frantic than ever. He just let the tide carry him along for a while as he tried to get his bearings. There were too many people to put his board down and cruise. But after four blocks he knew he wasn't getting anywhere. So he just stopped, mid-stride.

A woman in high heels ran into the back of him. A guy in a brown raincoat fell into her. The man apologized to the woman. She ignored him completely and told Gary, "Watch where you're going!"

Gary pulled himself over toward the buildings and stepped into the entranceway of a run-down office building. There was an old guy conked out and lying down on the concrete. His body was curled up and he held a bottle nestled into his chest. Nobody walking by was paying any attention to him. Gary just sat down on the steps beside the huddled figure.

The man had an old army coat over maybe ten layers of shirts. He had a blue wool cap pulled down over his ears and his shoes were worn through on the bottom, the laces untied. As Gary watched the man, he decided that he wasn't breathing. The guy must be dead.

Gary reached over and gently tapped the shoulder. Nothing. He had never seen a dead person up close before. God, this was awful. He tugged a little harder at the arm. What on earth would he do with a dead man? *Something had to be done*. Hundreds of people were still streaming by on the sidewalk but no one else was interested. Gary stared at the dead man.

Suddenly the head shook and the eyes opened. Gary squelched a scream. The old man didn't. He looked Gary straight in the eye and yelled, "You can't have it. It's mine!"

With that, he tucked the empty bottle tighter in to his chest and got on his feet. He glared at Gary and then pushed himself out into the crowd. As he stumbled off, he began an angry argument with no one. His voice rose above the street noises and the pedestrians instinctively moved out of his way to let him pass.

Gary was alone in the doorway. The place smelled awful. He got up to leave and allowed himself to again be carried along with the crowd. Sheila had led him around the city before. She understood the streets.

He only had a vague idea where KTV was located but he was pretty sure he was on the right street. Even if he got there, he doubted that they'd let him in. He doubted that he could even have a chance to talk to Kelly Merrill. It was completely hopeless, but completely necessary.

He walked on for a few blocks and then he saw it. Across the street was a tall, dark, glass building. It looked mysterious and very important. In orange letters above the first floor doorway he saw it: KTV. Gary knew what he had to do. He started across the street. A taxi screeched to a halt as he sprinted forward without looking. The driver shook a fist at him through the windshield and Gary brought his own fist down hard on the hood of the cab. Then he ran for the building before the driver had a chance to get out and start cursing at him.

Gary pushed his way through the revolving door and into the lobby. A security guard spotted him immediately and came forward. "Can I help you?" he asked in a cold, formal voice.

"I'd like to see Kelly, Kelly Merrill. She's a reporter."

"Yes, I know. Please ask at the desk."

Gary walked across the stone floor of the hollow, echoing lobby and told the woman at the switchboard that he was here to see Kelly Merrill.

"Do you have an appointment?"

"No," Gary said, then added, "but she'll be expecting me. The name is Gary Sutherland."

"Have a seat, Mr. Sutherland. I'll see if she's available."

Gary sat down and waited. When he became impatient, he went back to the switchboard operator. "Well?"

"Well," she said, "Ms. Merrill said that she might be down and for you to wait if you wanted to. She is in the middle of production."

"The witch," Gary said under his breath. He took a seat again and leafed through a copy of *People* magazine. It was full of smiling, successful celebrities. He didn't believe the smiles. And he wondered if all the stories were lies.

An elevator door opened and Kelly walked out. She walked straight toward him. Gary hadn't really looked at her before. She was strikingly beautiful, so beautiful that it scared him.

"You came to see me," she said. "I think I know why. Come on, let's go up to my desk."

Gary said nothing. He followed her into the elevator and watched as she pushed the eleventh floor. The door opened and she led him down a carpeted hallway, past teletype machines and video monitors. He passed a wall of TV screens, a different

station on each one. He was ready to
chicken out. Who was he to be telling a big
TV station that they were a pack of liars
and cheats?

"Sit down."

There was someone else in the room. She
stood up as he entered.

"Sheila!"

Sheila smiled at him. "I guess we both
had the same idea, huh?"

Gary grinned. "Yeh, I guess we did." The
world started to make some sense to him
again. Sheila was mad too. She had cut
school to come down here to complain.
Gary sat down beside her.

Kelly studied his face. "Sheila has already explained some things to me. I
think I know why you're here." She didn't
seem like the cool, matter-of-fact reporter
who had interviewed him yesterday.

"You saw the report?" she asked.

"You tricked us," Gary blurted out. "You
changed the whole story. You cut off the
important stuff I had to say and you made
us look like fools."

Kelly had turned professional at the sign
of anger. "You have to understand.
There's an editing process..."

"Bull. That wasn't editing. That
was...cheating." He wasn't sure he knew
what editing was but he knew that whatever had happened, it wasn't fair.

"What you did on the news simply wasn't fair," Sheila added. "You made skateboarders look like monsters, and you made the creep, Rinehart, look good."

"Look, I have people I'm responsible to. This is my job. I cover the story the way I see it and then they add to it...or change it or use just a part of my interview. That's the way TV news works."

She was pulling an adult trip on him. He hated that. *When you're older, you'll understand.* He could hear the echo of his mother.

Gary was smouldering. He looked hard at her. The fact that she was beautiful made him hate her even more. "Witch!" he said, this time out loud. He got up and turned to leave. Sheila was right behind him.

"Wait!" Kelly said. She jumped up and walked to the door of her small cubicle office. She touched Gary on the shoulder, sat him down and closed the door.

"You're right to be angry with me." She had turned back into a human being. "That wasn't the way the story was supposed to turn out. I went there to do *your* story, the one explained to me by Sheila on the phone the other night."

"But what happened?" Sheila asked.

"What happened was television."

"What do you mean?"

81

"Somebody over my head said to change the slant of the story. I was handed some statistics about skateboard injuries. Research dug up some file footage of kids in hospitals. I said I wanted to scrap the whole piece, but we had five minutes to fill, and our story had to go on the air."

"Most kids get banged up from skateboarding in parking lots or on the streets," Gary told her. "I'm not saying that the pool was one hundred percent safe but we would go along with whatever the town wants to do to make it safer."

"That might be true," she said, "but a lot of people think skateboarding is downright dangerous. Some people here at the station convinced me that Rinehart had a good point, that he was looking out for the welfare of kids in the community. So that's what we went with."

"That's a load of boloney and you know it." Sheila was defiant. The old Sheila had returned.

"It's just the way it works."

"Well I think it stinks," Gary answered. He and Sheila got up to go.

"I'll lead you out," Kelly said.

"We'll find our way," Gary stated and closed the door hard behind them as they left. The newsroom was a flurry of excitement. A reporter was sprinting past him in the hallway. "A guy just jumped from a tower over on Sixty-ninth," he said to no one in particular. "We got the whole thing, top to bottom. It's just perfect."

Gary and Sheila opened the door to the elevator and got in. The door closed and they started to descend.

Chapter Eleven

Skate and Destroy

" I'm sorry, Gary," said Sheila, taking his arm as they came out of the revolving door. "I guess I screwed things up instead of making them better."

"No, at least you tried. I was really worried. I mean, when you didn't show up at the Grave and then I called and you didn't talk to me, I thought your parents finally got to you. I thought it was the end of us."

"Well, we do have a big problem. I'm not supposed to see you. My parents think you're nothing but trouble."

"I have a feeling they're right," Gary admitted.

"Well, I had to come down here today. I couldn't let them get away with those lies."

"Yeah, me too. But now you're in trouble, too. You cut school. Your parents will find out."

"Nah, don't worry. I've got a way around it. And now you and I have a whole day to goof-off downtown."

"What do you want to do?"

"I don't know. Let's just walk around. You got your board. Maybe we can find some new spots."

"OK." Gary felt a little lighter. It would be like old times. He'd forget about all the hassles for a while. It was just him and Sheila. Gary saw a side street sloping off down a hill. There was no traffic and just a couple of warehouses that looked empty. "Hop on," he said.

"Sure, let's go."

Together they sailed down the street, making gentle cutbacks as Gary avoided rocks and busted glass. He noticed the walls of the buildings, spray-painted with the words, "Skate and Destroy." What the heck was that supposed to mean? Skate and destroy what?

At the bottom of the hill, they walked on until they found another backstreet and another descent. "Here we go again," he said. He and Sheila cruised further on. It was a run-down part of town but that made it seem even more adventurous.

Suddenly six skateboarders came shooting into the street from an alleyway up ahead. One of them had a giant ghetto-blaster up to his ear. Gary cranked the board to a halt. He hoped they didn't see the two of them. These skatedogs looked like mean characters with a purpose.

"C'mon, let's get out of here." He picked up his board, grabbed Sheila's elbow and began to lead her back up the street. Too late. They had been spotted.

Somebody was whistling a loud piercing note, then, "Hey, skatefreak, identify!"

Gary suddenly got the picture...the Skate and Destroyers.

Gary's instincts told him to run, to get out of there. But there were six of them. There wouldn't be much chance of escape. "Stay here," he told Sheila. He hopped on his board and rolled toward them, expecting the worst.

The Skate and Destroyers were into black leather cut-off jackets and ripped clothing. "Welcome to the neighbourhood," a kid with a puffy smile and rotten teeth said to him.

"Nice place you have here," Gary said, looking around at the overturned garbage cans and the newspapers blowing around the street.

"We're just out for a little entertainment. Maybe you wanna join?" They all leered at him, and made a point of wrenching their necks to get a good look at Sheila. He could tell they wanted to eat him alive.

"I got business," Gary said, trying to sound tough. His voice cracked.

"What kind of business?"

"It's just something my girl and I are trying to figure out."

They snickered. "Yeah, like maybe we can help." They laughed long and hard. This was their scene. You could tell they played it before.

"Well, I got to go," Gary said. He knew they weren't going to let him off the hook.

"Wait," said the puffy-faced guy. He rolled on his board to within inches of Gary, then leaning toward him and breathing bad breath all over him, said "You good at dog fights?"

"I don't know what you mean."

"You can't be a real skatefreak if you ain't done dogfights. C'mon."

Gary was ready to split, but he was surrounded. He wanted to yell to Sheila to run, but it was a long empty street. He couldn't take the chance. Besides, he knew Sheila. She wouldn't run. Then they'd both be in a fix. He saw no way out. He waved for Sheila to join him. Sheila played it tough. She looked like she wasn't afraid of anybody. They led Gary and Sheila down a grungy side street to a small parking lot behind a paint factory. The lot was littered with busted beer bottles and old rusty car parts. Two of the kids went over to a shed leaning against the building and brought out four sheets of plywood.

The plywood was set up on a tilt with cement blocks. There was one sheet at each corner of a square. "Waddya think?" Puffy Face asked.

The pavement within the square was mined with pieces of broken bottles and scrap metal. "Interesting," Gary said, not wanting to sound like a wimp.

"Give it a try."

OK, Gary figured. No sweat. He'd show them what he could do. He pushed into the jury-rigged arena and shot from one side to the other. It was hard to keep an eye on the Skate and Destroyers while trying to impress them. All he could see was a blur. It seemed unreal, like he had arrived on another planet. His new chums clearly looked like aliens. But he did his best. He avoided a broken bottle, boomeranged from one side to the other, pulled off a 360 in the centre and carved turn after turn. Finally he was rolling up one of the sheets of plywood when two of the goons pulled the blocks out from under. He crashed down onto the flat ground and right into Puffy Face who was standing there waiting.

"That's just show-off stuff. I can see you're ready for the real thing," he told

Gary. "Check this out." Puffboy nodded his head to two of his henchmen who pushed into the arena. They skated up and down, back and forth, just like Gary had done but with a difference. They crossed directly back and forth trying to knock each other off with flailing fists.

Finally the shorter kid of the two ducked real low as he approached his adversary. He rammed his head straight into the belly of the oncoming skateboarder and they both fell to the pavement. The short guy was on top. So he won.

"Looks like fun to me," Gary said, his acting career off to an unhealthy start.

"Let's do it then," said the pack leader who, just now, looked a lot like the Pillsbury Doughboy. He tried to look at Sheila, but Sheila just gave him a hard, cold stare. She didn't say a word. It was then that Gary noticed the rings. The Doughboy wore ten shiny rings, one at each knuckle, and on each ring there was a tiny pyramid. He looked deadly as he pushed off with a heavy kick of his black boot. He shoved his weight forward and back, getting speed up for the back and forth assault. But he looked uncomfortable on the board. His weight was against him.

Gary, skinny and agile, threw himself into the action but keeping only on the defensive. He played it for speed—fast and low. He'd see the fist coming at him and he'd duck. He saw the monster moving in for the kill from behind him and he'd carve hard on the rail and zip up the ramp. His heart pounded wildly. The S and D boys hooted and laughed but Gary knew they weren't going to let him off easy. He'd have to do more than just elude the Doughboy. He'd go for speed and surprise. He pushed even harder off the pavement; he kicked wild, in-the-air turns off the ramps. The Doughboy was right on his tail now, ready to grab him around the neck and whip him backwards. Gary ducked again, carved right, pulled a 180 on the ramp and came down behind his opponent. He followed him up one ramp, then passed him and began a mad charge from one side to another, keeping a clear distance between them.

Then, as a complete surprise to the goon, Gary zipped up close behind and yanked the board out from behind him. Puffy Face launched forward. His forehead hit the pavement first, as he skidded to a stop.

Gary kicked up his own board and stopped dead in his tracks. He was ready to run now but only as a last resort. He hated this scene.

Gary walked over to the victim and tried to help him up, but he was pushed away.

The Doughboy was turning over and getting up. He had scraped his forehead pretty bad and it was bleeding. A thick hand dabbed at the blood and held it up in front of his eyes.

"I'm sorry," Gary said.

The hand felt the blood again. Suddenly the Doughboy's face cracked into a smile. "Not bad," he said. "Not bad at all." The guys laughed.

"Wanna go at it again?" the Doughboy asked, his face lit up in a maniacal smile.

"No thanks," Gary said. "I got business."

"Oh yeah, business. OK, go do your business. Maybe we try again tomorrow, eh?"

"Sure, anytime." Gary smiled. He and Sheila turned their backs on the Skate and Destroyers and began to walk away ever so slowly. He expected any second to be grabbed from behind and nailed to the ground. He expected to wake up in the morning bleeding into some trash can. He refused to think about what might happen to Sheila. But nothing happened. They walked on around uphill until they were back on a busy sidewalk, not saying a word.

Then Sheila spoke. "That was a close call."

"I had it all under control. No sweat." Gary was still faking confidence.

"Liar," Sheila said, elbowing him in the ribs until he fell over laughing. People on the street stopped and looked at them. Sheila helped Gary back up onto his feet. "Well, that explains one thing, anyway."

"What's that?" Gary asked.

"Well, it explains why skateboarders have such a bad reputation in the city. If there are many more of those creeps around, it's no wonder adults think skateboarders are criminals."

Gary could see her point. He was beginning to see that he didn't have a prayer in winning his battle to save the Grave.

Chapter Twelve

The New Rules

On the bus back to Riverdale, Sheila and Gary sat way in the back. Gary had his arm around her.

"Gary, I've got to get to the school by 3:15."

"You've gotta be kidding. Why?"

"Because my mother's picking me up. It's part of her new rules. She thinks that if she picks me up right after school, I can't hang around with you. She's very serious about it."

"How are you gonna change her mind? We can't keep hiding from her forever."

"I don't know. We'll work something out. You're going to have to prove to her you're not a troublemaker."

"I guess I'm doing a great job of that." Gary sounded defeated. He held Sheila tighter, tried to figure out how he was going to win the approval of her parents.

They got off the bus and ran to the school, arriving just minutes before the final bell rang. They saw Sheila's mom driving up the school driveway. Gary said goodbye and slinked off toward the side of the building. He was walking backwards, still looking at Sheila and not watching where he was going when he bumped into someone.

He turned around. It was the Faulk.

"I want to see you in my office, mister. And I mean now." Gary knew he was in deep muck.

He followed Faulkner to the outer office where he was directed to a chair and told to wait.

"Get me Gary Sutherland's father on the phone," Faulkner told the secretary.

"Right away, sir," she said.

But Gary never heard the conversation. The Faulk had retreated to his office and closed the door. Nothing happened. Ten minutes passed. Then twenty. Then his old man appeared in the doorway. He looked like he was ready to explode.

Faulkner opened his door. "Thanks for coming, Mr. Sutherland. Both of you, please come in."

Doom. Gary felt like he had just been sentenced to life imprisonment in an underground pit.

"Mr. Sutherland, your son was not in school today. Do you have any idea why?"

"No. Maybe he would like to explain."

Gary tried to think up some convincing, fantastic lie, something that they would both buy. He rummaged through the closets of his brain, but there was nothing they would believe. He gave it his best shot.

"I was abducted by aliens. Right in front of the school this morning."

"Gary!" his father growled.

Gary decided there was nothing to do but tell the truth. So far the truth had got him into nothing but trouble, but he was a lousy liar. He explained first to Faulkner about the Grave and about the news last night.

"I saw it," Faulkner said. "I had the feeling that something was missing in the story. I don't think they gave you fair coverage." He looked down at the lines in his hands, almost as if he were reading something. "But that still doesn't mean you can get away with a locker filled with garbage, missed detentions and cutting school." There, the list of his crimes had been set down. "I've suspended students for less."

"Gary, I had no idea you were getting yourself into such a mess. What are we going to do with you?" his father said.

"Before we decide that," the Faulk cut in, "I want to try and understand why this is so important...this business over the swimming pool...I want to try to understand why your son thinks this is worth risking his school career over."

It was like Gary's mom had said. He was "ruining his life."

Before Gary had a chance to talk, his father spoke. "In a way, I think I can understand how Gary feels. He thinks that kids shouldn't be kicked around when it comes to things they care about. Like skateboarding. In one respect, I'm on his side. The city shouldn't be taking away the pool unless they are going to replace it with something else. Now, the kids have no place to go but back into the streets or in parking lots. It's just not safe."

Gary couldn't believe his ears.

Faulkner looked intensely interested. "Go on."

"I don't know if I should share this with you, but I made a phone call to the city planning office today. I asked why the land was being sold to a private developer and how much the city would get for it. I was told that the city needed more revenue to 'cover deficits.' That didn't help me much. But then the guy told me the price that Langille Brothers have offered to pay for it."

"Yes?" The Faulk was leaning forward, keenly interested now.

"The price was really very low."

Gary couldn't quite put it all together. Why had his old man bothered to make the phone calls? And why on earth did he see a glimmer in the eyes of his school principal?

"I don't know exactly what's going on, but I don't like the feel of it."

"Calvin Rinehart was never one of my favourite people, Mr. Sutherland, but I don't know if he's capable of what you're suggesting."

Gary didn't exactly know what his old man had suggested.

"But I did see him on TV last night," the Faulk continued. "And I knew enough about the pool business to realize that he was manipulating the TV people. I felt badly for the kids."

"I plan on going to the city council meeting next week. I just want to ask a few questions."

"I think that's wise of you. I wish you luck." Faulkner took a deep breath. "But meanwhile, what are we going to do with this difficult son of yours?"

"Whatever you think is suitable," Gary's father said. "He certainly isn't off the hook. He deserves punishment."

"I'm thinking of three weeks of detention. He's going to need the time to catch up on schoolwork anyway."

"I accept," Gary said. He wanted to be co-operative. He really did. In fact, he was so excited by his father's new interest in the Grave that the idea of detention didn't bother him at all.

"You know you're getting off easy. But I have to add one more thing. I want to see that locker of yours clean and orderly, you understand?"

"Yes, sir.

At school the next day, Howie and Richard caught up with Gary as he was entering home room. "Man, you shoulda been there," Howie said.

"Been where?" Gary asked.

"At Rinehart's house," Blades explained. "We sneaked over there and let the air out of all his tires. It was the revenge of the skatedogs."

"That was a stupid thing to do."

"Stupid, huh," Blades snapped back. "Wait'll you see what we have planned for that TV lady and her film crew."

Gary thought about his meeting with Kelly Merrill. Yeah, maybe she did deserve a few of Blades' and Meeker's pranks. But he also knew that these guys were playing right into Rinehart's hands.

They'd get caught and then they'd all just look like a bunch of juvenile delinquents.

"Don't be stupid. That stuff isn't going to do any good."

"Oh yeah," Richard said. "Just wait until we dump black paint into Rinehart's new, heated swimming pool. The guy's rich. He can afford a little damage."

"Count me out of it."

"Chicken?" Blades asked, dropping his sunglasses back on so they slid halfway down his nose.

Gary just shook his head. The bell rang for homeroom. "Hey, wait a minute. Richard, how much do you think a mayor makes a year?"

Blades and Meeker just laughed. "Who knows? What does it matter anyway?"

As they walked away from him, something began to fit together in Gary's mind.

Chapter Thirteen

Not Over Yet

At first Gary thought his old man was going to be easy on him. Maybe his father really did understand his problem. But it wasn't quite like he hoped. His parents monitored his every move.

He had to come right home after detention. He wasn't allowed out at night. And he had to show his parents every bit of homework he did each day. It was a real drag, like being twelve years old again. But, worst of all, he could only talk to Sheila during lunch and between classes at school. And he couldn't possibly sneak into the Grave for a session.

But his old man was serious about the city council meeting. He had phoned up some of the other parents; they had all said they were too busy, or that they weren't interested or that it wasn't any of their business. All except for Sheila's mother. She promised to show up at the council meeting. "But I'll only be there to listen," she said. "I don't have anything that I want to say about it."

On the night of the meeting, Gary and his parents sat way in the back of the hall. He saw Sheila and her mother sitting down front. Maybe there was hope for them yet. Faulkner was also there, sitting by himself, half dozing.

After a long, boring debate over property taxes, his father finally had a chance to go the front and ask about the pool. His father looked very nervous.

"I'd like to ask Mr. Rinehart about the land of the old Centennial Pool that is soon to be developed for a shopping mall."

Rinehart looked at the other city councillors sitting around him. Then he gave a rather disgusted look to Mr. Sutherland. "I'm afraid you're wasting this council's time. That matter has been discussed long ago. An option has been offered and accepted by the developer. It's no longer a matter that's open for discussion."

Gary's father looked flustered. "But as a tax-paying citizen of this city, I feel it's only fair that you answer a few of my questions." His voice warbled a little but there was genuine anger in it as well.

Rinehart was annoyed. "I'm sorry, but you really would be wasting our time. The decision has been made...democratically by a vote of city councillors. You really should have come around then. Would you mind relinquishing the floor to the next person?"

Gary's father looked stunned. He hadn't even had a chance to ask a question. Gary's mother squirmed uncomfortably in her seat. Gary realized something. Rinehart had just pulled an adult trip on his own father. He had given his old man one of those looks that said, 'You don't know anything about it. We do. So why don't you just be quiet.'

Then someone else stood up. It was Mrs. Holman.

"Mr. Rinehart, I don't think you can just cut off this gentleman who has a legitimate concern for the young people in the community."

Now Rinehart seemed a little more than just mildly annoyed now. "Look, if you both think that I should give into the demands of those young hoodlums on skateboards, you're wrong. Would you like me to bring forward some of the police officers from this city who have arrested young punks on skateboards who break the law every day in this city? I think that if you heard some of the stories, neither of you would be willing to defend them."

"But I'm not just talking about skate-boarding," Gary's dad now objected. "I'm talking about taking away public land, a swimming pool, and not providing any replacement, anything for recreation for kids in the community."

"Sir, we do have plans to replace the pool. It'll be an indoor pool. Now can't we move along?" The other councillors all shuffled their papers. They too seemed annoyed with Gary's dad.

"On what land are you going to build the new pool?" his dad shouted.

"That's yet to be decided," Rinehart responded.

"But why not keep the old property and let it be used for a skateboard park, at least until the new pool is ready to be built."

"My good sir, the land has, for all intents and purposes been sold. There is a binding legal document. The matter is closed."

Sheila's mother was on her feet again. "Why not answer his question?" she said.

Gary's father was not ready to give up the floor. "And what about the price the city is being paid for the land? You'll never be able to buy another lot that size for such a pittance. The land is as good as given away for the price Langille paid for it."

Rinehart motioned to a police officer by the back door. He walked forward and touched Mr. Sutherland's elbow. Gary's mother looked like she was about to go into shock.

Mrs. Holman, still on her feet, shouted to the mayor, "Is what he says true? What about the price of the land?" Gary's father was being led quietly out of the room.

Rinehart, composing himself now that he realized he had regained control, said simply, "The land was offered at a fair market price and we found a willing buyer. I think that's all there is to it, thank you." And then the councillors were on to other business as if this had never happened.

Gary knew that his mother was embarrassed. "C'mon, let's go," he said. They got up to leave and he saw Sheila looking back at him. She was moving her lips without speaking. It took her three tries but the message finally sunk in: "It's not over yet," she said.

On the way home, Gary's father was boiling mad. "The man humiliated me," he said.

"What else can we do?" Gary asked.

"Nothing," his mother said. "Now can we just forget about it? Your father has other things to worry about."

"Don't tell me what I have to worry about," his old man said. Now he was yelling. Gary decided to keep his mouth shut.

Chapter Fourteen

Fat Cats and Shopping Malls

During detention the next day, Gary was shocked to see Sheila sitting there beside him.

"What are you doing here?"

"Shh." She took out a piece of paper and wrote him a note: "This was the only way I could spend more time with you."

Gary smiled, wrote back, "Thanks."

Mrs. Stephano was up front, reading *Newsweek* magazine. As long as the room was quiet, she didn't bother to look up.

"There's more…." she wrote.

"What?" he whispered.

"LET'S GET RINEHART!" she wrote in big bold letters.

"Sure, but how?" he wrote back.

"Research," she responded and underlined it three times.

Gary shrugged his shoulders. He wasn't quite sure what she meant. Whatever it was, it made more sense than black paint poured into Rinehart's swimming pool.

At the end of detention, Sheila walked with Gary to the front of the school. Her mother was sitting in her car waiting to pick Sheila up. "I still can't let her see you with me," she said, pulling him back into the hallway.

"I thought she was on our side now," Gary said.

"It's not that simple. She still doesn't trust you."

Gary hung his head.

"But things are going to change. Listen. Do you know what your father was getting at last night?"

"Yeah, he was really mad that kids don't have anything to do around here."

"But I think there was more. Remember him asking about the price of the land?"

"Yeah, so?"

"So, it got me thinking. Rinehart might be a crook. Did your father suggest anything about that?"

"No, he didn't want to talk about anything after the meeting. He was pretty upset. Somehow I think it was all my fault."

"Don't be stupid. It's not your fault. But I think your father had a hunch. There's something funny about the land deal."

Now the light bulbs started going on. "So there might be a real way to nail Rinehart for what he did to us? Like if he had a deal with the developer, or something?"

"Only research will tell."

Gary looked thoughtful. "Sheila, how much do you think a mayor earns? His salary, I mean?"

"I don't know. Why don't you call his office and ask."

"You mean I can do that?"

"It's public information. Just say you're doing a research project for school. Put together his salary and his millionaire's residence, and maybe that's where the deal looks crooked. Is that what your Dad is getting at?"

With that Sheila rushed away to her mother's car.

Gary walked straight home. It was after four o'clock. The day was shot. No more hanging out with the guys, no more skateboarding. He sat down in front of the TV but there was nothing on but soap operas. He turned it off and sat staring at the phone. He decided it was time to do a little research.

A secretary answered in the mayor's office.

"I'm doing a research project in school on municipal government. I wonder if you could tell me something about exactly what a mayor does." Gary tried to sound like a real egghead.

"Well, it's rather complicated but hold on, I have a book around here that gives some of the specifics." Gary listened as she rattled on about official ceremonies and meetings and budgets.

"That's very helpful, thanks. I have just one more question. Could you tell me what the salary is for the job?"

She gave him the answer he was looking for. "I appreciate that so much. Thank you. Goodbye."

He looked at the figure he had written down on a piece of paper. It was about the same amount as his father made a year. Gary wondered about the fancy new house, the two car garage and the heated swimming pool. How had Rinehart become such a fat cat on such an average salary? He couldn't wait to tell Sheila.

Then next morning in school, he told her the findings of his research. She didn't seem surprised at all.

"Are you ready for this ?" she asked.

"I'm ready for anything."

"I phoned some real estate people about our street, and the neighbourhood and I described Rinehart's house. They both said that they thought it was worth about half a million bucks. And you know, he even has a hot tub in that glass room, right off the sunken living-room."

"I also asked one guy about the value of a piece of property like the old pool grounds. He said he could only make a rough guess, but since there was so little land of that size left in Riverdale, he figured it was worth well over a million."

"But my father told me the city only got a quarter of that."

"Precisely."

"But I still can't fit all the pieces together."

"Then listen to the rest. The last guy I phoned, John Martin, wanted to be really helpful. I think he liked my voice. I gave him the details on the house. He kept asking me questions and I tried to describe the place as best as I could. So then he says, 'Oh, you mean a place just like the one Calvin Rinehart moved into, the one in the subdivision developed by the Langilles?' I said, 'Yes, that's the one.' And he too told me it was worth about a half a million dollars. But do you see what's beginning to connect?"

"I sure do," Gary said. "Rinehart probably did some kind of a deal so that the Langille Brothers got the land for their shopping mall cheap."

"And Calvin Rinehart got himself an extra-special good deal on a new home."

"But how are we going to prove it?"

"I don't know," Sheila said. "Let's talk to your father about it."

"Good idea."

The bell was about to ring. Gary saw Howie Blades walking toward them, his head hanging down like he had just been beaten up. "Howie, man, we figured out a way to get back at Rinehart."

"Forget it man. Leave me out of it."

"Why? You were the one out for revenge."

"Well, we tried, old buddy. And got caught."

"Oops."

"Oops is right. Meeker and me got the paint in the pool all right but we never got back over the fence. It's gonna cost us big bucks to clean it up."

Chapter Fifteen

Parent Power

After dinner, when Gary's father answered the door, he was more than a little startled to find Sheila and her mother. "May we come in?" Mrs. Holman asked.

"Sure," Gary's dad said. "It's nice to see you." But something in his voice suggested he was worried. Mrs. Sutherland came into the room with Gary and, for a minute, an awkward silence hung in the room. The three adults seemed mildly embarrassed. Sheila looked at Gary and gave him a wink.

"Would you like some coffee, Mrs. Holman?" Gary's mom asked.

"Yes, that would be fine, thanks."

Mr. Sutherland was a white as a ghost. Gary suddenly had the feeling that his old man thought Sheila was pregnant. It looked like that sort of a scene.

"Perhaps I should explain," Sheila began.

"Maybe you should," said Mr. Sutherland, sinking back into a chair.

"Gary and I did a little digging," Sheila explained. "Rinehart sold the land too cheap. The city's been ripped off."

"And Rinehart is living in this big new house that he shouldn't be able to afford," Gary blurted out.

Sheila filled in more of the details.

"None of this surprises me," said Gary's father. "What you found out, that is. Still, it would take much more research than this to make a case for newspaper headlines reading 'Corruption in City Hall.' He could have inherited some money to build himself a big mansion. Maybe he sold his business, the paint store on Mountain Road, and made a bundle that way."

"Maybe he's in with the Mafia," interrupted Gary.

"So what can we do now?" said Sheila.

Gary's father continued. "I know a reporter at the *Star* who is doing some stories about City Hall. He may well be interested in these facts, and this story. He can probably put something together, do some more research and maybe he'll help to make public some things that Calvin Rinehart would rather not have put in print."

"What about the woman at KTV?" asked Mrs. Holman. "She may also be interested in these new bits of information, and about our treatment at the Council meeting the other night."

"Yeah, I'll go call her right away. Give her a chance to get the record straight."

"Wait a minute, Sheila," said Mr. Sutherland. "Why don't I drive you and Gary downtown tomorrow morning. I'll take the morning off work. You can go to school in the afternoon. We'll go to both KTV and the *Star*. Anyway, I am curious now. I'd like to get to the bottom of this whole swimming pool affair."

Gary and Sheila exchanged looks of utter disbelief.

The next day Kelly Merrill was surprised to see the return of Sheila and Gary. Gary's father introduced himself.

"I'm just along for the ride," he said and settled back into a chair while Gary and Sheila made their pitch.

Sheila told Kelly their discoveries about Rinehart, his house, the land deal, the meeting at City Hall, leaving out nothing. Kelly listened attentively but didn't reveal her own thoughts. Gary was sure she was going to send them packing. He was sure she would think they made it all up just to get back at Rinehart. But the clincher was that his old man was there.

It made them look like they had their act together.

"What do you two want out of this?" asked Kelly.

"We want Rinehart to get what's coming to him," Sheila said.

"We want the Grave back," said Gary at the same time.

"I can't promise anything. But I think you have a lot of guts to come to me with this and I'll give it my best shot."

"Yeah, but how do we know we can trust you?" Gary asked, still a little sceptical. "Last time you made us look like delinquents."

"You know, Gary, I thought the display was impressive. Dangerous, but impressive. I still have the original film we taped. I'll see what develops with this story. We'll have to do some research of our own."

The three visitors left the TV station and went over to the newspaper offices. Mr. Sutherland spent a few minutes with a reporter. When they left, he told Sheila and Gary that all they could do now was wait and see.

Two days later, on Friday, Sheila was waiting for Gary as he arrived at school. She was holding the morning paper opened to a story on page three, "Developer gets sweetheart deal on Centennial Pool."

Gary grabbed the corner of the paper. Soon Meeker and Blades joined them.

"Listen to this," cried Gary. " 'Mayor Rinehart's half-million dollar residence in the subdivision recently developed by Bob Langille's firm, is a high-class home for the man who calls himself "the working-person's mayor." In a recent interview he said, "I am interested in doing what is best for the people in my community." The mayor's office denies any connection between his elegant Langille-built home, complete with heated swimming pool, hot tub, two-car garage and the sweet land deal which will put $250,000 in city coffers, for a site valued at 4 times that amount.'"

"It's all there," exclaimed Sheila. "Right in the paper. This'll make waves!"

"Hey, good stuff," said Blades.

"Let's show the Faulk," said Gary. "He seems to have something in for Rinehart."

That was Friday morning. By Friday night Gary and Sheila had given up on a replay from KTV, and it didn't look as if they could "Save the Grave" with one newspaper article.

Chapter Sixteen

Say Goodbye to the Grave

At nine o'clock on Saturday morning, Gary was lying in bed feeling sorry for himself. Nothing was working out. And then the phone rang. It was Blades.

"I just saw two trucks pull into the Grave towing flatbeds with bulldozers on them. This is it. The end of the Grave." Blades sounded frantic. "There's a couple of dump trucks there, too filled with rocks. It's all over."

"No, it can't be. Not yet. Meet me there in ten minutes. Bring your parents. Tell them it's an emergency." Gary slammed down the phone. It couldn't happen like this. He was so close to winning. Now he'd lose it all.

In desperation, he tried KTV again. He asked for Kelly. Miraculously she was in. Gary explained the situation.

"I'll be there as quick as I can," she said and hung up.

Gary dialled again. His brain was working like rapid fire. "They're about to fill in the Grave, Sheila. We have to move fast. Call Meeker, Wiser, Jones and anybody else you think can help. Tell them to get over there and make sure they bring their parents. We can't do this alone."

"I'll do what I can."

Gary threw on his clothes that were left lying in the middle of the floor. His feet found their way into his running shoes and he flew downstairs where his parents were eating a leisurely breakfast.

"The Grave. We have to get over there now. They're filling it in." Gary grabbed his board from the corner. His parents followed him outside. In seconds they were in the car and out of the driveway.

Neither of his parents said a word. His father drove like a maniac and his mom bit hard on her lip.

Gary didn't want it to end like this. Not now, not before they'd had a chance to tell their side, a chance to Save the Grave.

Mr. Sutherland parked on the street. A few other cars were stopping as well. Kids were getting out. Kids with skateboards. Part of the chain-link fence had been torn down where the old entrance to the pool grounds used to be. One of the dump trucks had already emptied a load of stones near the edge of the pool. Another was about to back in. There was a bull-dozer in the parking lot but the driver seemed to be having trouble getting it un-loaded from the flatbed trailer.

The parents got out of their cars and looked at each other.

"What are we doing here, anyway?" Wiser's old man asked.

Gary's father answered, "I think we're trying to save the pool." He started to ex-plain about Rinehart. "Help me out with this, Gary," he said turning to his son. But his son wasn't there.

Gary was running toward the torn-out section of the fence. The second truck had just emptied a load of rocks near the edge and pulled away. The bulldozer was off the flatbed now and crawling toward the pool.

Blades, Meeker, Wiser, Jones and Gary were standing in front of the gaping hole in the fence. They held their boards across their chests. The bulldozer was creeping straight towards them. The driver was yelling at them, waving his hand for them to get out of the way.

All at once the parents began to run to-wards their kids. They were shouting for them to move but the guys just shook their heads, no. Together, the boys began to chant, "Save the Grave!" Out of the corner of his eye, Gary saw a lone skatedog running toward the pumphouse across the pool. Everything was happening at once.

The parents made their way to the kids as the bulldozer crept closer. "Get out of the way!" Mrs. Meeker screamed.

"We're not moving," Meeker shouted back to his mother.

"This is crazy," Wiser's old man yelped.

"Maybe it isn't crazy. Maybe it's important," Gary heard his father say. The bulldozer was just ten feet from where they all stood. The driver looked furious.

"Get out of the way or I'll run you all over," he screamed.

Wiser's old man yelled back to him, "Hey, buddy, who the hell do you think you are?"

The driver revved the engine loud as if he was ready to advance, but the machine didn't move.

Gary saw Rinehart's car pulling up the driveway. This time he had *three* cop cars with him.

"I don't believe this," Mr. Sutherland said. He looked at his son. Gary just shrugged his shoulders.

The police cars drove up over the curb and directly alongside of the bulldozer. Six cops got out very slowly, each carrying a night stick. Foster walked up to Mr.

Sutherland who had stepped forward to meet them.

"I have no idea what this is all about, mister," Foster said, "but I think the first thing you all need to do is get out of the way and let that man do his job."

"We just want this delayed for a few days," Mr. Sutherland said. "Just until the whole story is out."

Foster ignored him. "Look, right now you're all trespassing and it's our job to have you removed or arrest all of you."

At the word "arrest" the other parents flinched. They began to pull their kids away. It was all over now. There was nothing they could do. Gary's father saw the others pulling their kids towards their cars. He looked at Gary and shook his head. "I'm sorry," he said.

Gary knew he was defeated. It had been a miracle that things had gone this far. They had been so close.

As soon as the people were out of the way, the police created a line between the 'dozer and the demonstrators. The driver immediately fired up his machine and pushed forward. He was about to force the massive pile of rocks into the pool. It would be the end of the Grave. Forever.

Suddenly somebody screamed out. "Stop!" A woman was running toward the police line. It was Mrs. Holman.

Gary saw something move over by the pumphouse on the far side of the pool. Someone was climbing over the fence. Someone with a skateboard. It was Sheila. Oh my God, Gary thought. There was no way to get past the cops. He ran for the fence closest to him and grappled to the top, cutting himself on the old rusty barbed wire that ripped through his shirt.

The bulldozer had connected with the pile of rocks. The driver gunned the engine, prepared to get it over with. But he didn't see Sheila on the other side of the pool. The pile was too high.

"No!" Gary yelled. He was caught on the wire at the top of the fence. He saw Sheila set her skateboard down on the lip of the pool. She placed her feet carefully and she dropped. Gary saw her glide down the steep side, almost perfect freefall, then compress herself as she hit the curved bottom of the pool.

The engine roared. The driver shoved at the pile of rock and the first stones began to fall into the pool. The police now saw Sheila. They yelled to the driver but he couldn't hear them. All at once, everyone was running toward the 'dozer.

Gary tore off his shirt and leaped over the fence. Sheila had crossed the bottom and was now shooting up the other side. Behind her rocks were raining down onto the concrete below. He prayed that she had the speed. Seconds stretched out like hours. He ran but his feet couldn't move fast enough.

And then Sheila was all the way up the side of the pool. She was in the air, hanging onto her board with one hand. She was maybe three feet above the rim. But she had lost it. And she was still directly above the pool. She was about to fall back into the Grave, a twenty-foot drop down onto a bottom littered now with jagged rocks.

Gary reached out a hand and grabbed Sheila by the wrist. He used all his strength to pull her over onto the concrete pavement as her board fell back down into the pool.

The guy in the bulldozer saw what happened. He stopped his machine. He turned it off.

"That's it," he said. "I'm gettin' out of here. No job is worth this." He started to walk away but looked around at the parents and kids that had gathered. "You people are crazy, you know that?" he said. "You're all completely out of your minds."

Escorted by Foster and Duck, Calvin Rinehart was now on the scene. He looked straight at Gary this time. "It's not going to work," he told him.

122

Gary was still hanging onto Sheila. They were both shaking from the near-tragedy. Gary couldn't speak. But someone had walked up behind him.

"What's not going to work, Mr. Rinehart?"

It was Kelly Merrill. She was holding out a microphone. The camera was right behind her.

Rinehart tried to compose himself. You could tell he hadn't figured on more media attention. He cleared his throat. "Because here in this city, law and order must prevail. We can't allow lunatic factions...children or adults...of the community to just break the law whenever they want to."

"But what about the laws on kickbacks and bribery, Mr. Mayor? Is there, by any chance, a connection between the sweet deal Langille got on this land...and the deal you got on your new house in one of their developments?"

Rinehart looked around him at the parents and their kids. He turned to the Foster, "Get all these people out of here," he snarled. "They're trespassing on private property."

But Foster shook his head. All six of the cops were staring at Rinehart.

"It's not private property," Gary's father told Rinehart. "It's public land. And it's going to stay that way."

Rinehart backed away from them and started walking toward his car.

"Stay with him," Kelly told her cameraman. "Keep it rolling until he's in the car and gone."

Blades and Meeker let out a whoop. Jones and Wiser had already climbed down the side of the Grave and were throwing rocks back up to the top. A couple of fathers climbed the old pool ladder down to the bottom and began to help.

"Their research was pretty good," Kelly told Sheila's mother. "Rinehart was pretty sloppy with his scheme. I have permission from my producer to run the story tonight. We're going to run a revised piece on skatedogs as well. But I'm still not sure it will save this place forever."

Suddenly for the first time all day, Gary was scared to death. He thought about Sheila, about grabbing her in mid-air before she fell back into the pool. Gary didn't care now if the Grave lasted forever. Maybe nothing lasted forever. Nothing but him and Sheila.